Speed

Black Hawk MC
Book One

by Carson Mackenzie

Published by CM Books, LLC

Cover Design by Carson Mackenzie

Synopsis

Kane "Speed" Weston, after leaving the military, returns to the Black Hawk MC, the club he grew up in, the only family he has left. With his father's spot open, he prepares to fill the position. What he finds upon his return, the military nor the MC could have prepared him for.

Sami Borelli was raised in an MC. With her father being the president of the club, she'd been referred to as a princess, feeling anything but. Sami moved to the Black Hawk MC's territory when her father's club faced internal problems, turning her into a liability instead of an asset. She met a man at a club party who changed her life, but when she went back, he was gone, only to return years later with no memory of her while she remembered everything about him.

The sons of the Black Hawk MC are home and ready to take the places within the club they were groomed for. What they were never taught was how to handle losing their hearts.

Table of Contents

Prologue

Speed

The only things noticeable on the isolated highway were the sounds of engines roaring and headlights gleaming. I turned my bike and headed down the exit ramp that read "Shades Valley 1.3m" to the left, with the other bikes following closely behind me. Our final destination—the town cemetery.

The bikes were parked, and the men dismounted, standing still as the hearse driver opened the back door revealing the casket inside. Six men stepped forward, each taking a handle on the coffin, hoisting it out of the vehicle as they walked slowly to the freshly dug grave. They set the casket down gently, each laying a palm flat on the lid, saying their individual goodbye to their brother before stepping back and taking their place with the others in the circle of men around the grave.

Our brother, Preacher, stepped forward to say the last words pertaining to the man inside the casket, their brother, their friend, and their comrade. To me, the man in the box was all those things and more—my dad, Harvey Weston. Better known as Cutter, one of the Enforcers of the Black Hawk MC. Each of us bowed our heads saying a silent goodbye to one of our own. After everything was done, we turned and headed to our bikes for the ride back to the clubhouse to celebrate the man who would no longer have a physical presence among us.

The clubhouse was in full swing with the hang-arounds and ol' ladies rushing around, setting out food, and stocking the bar for the celebration to begin upon our arrival. The women didn't attend the final service, it was for the men of the club, our final ride with our brother to say goodbye. The women attended the night before when the members from the other Charters came to pay their respect. Now, everyone would share in the party to remember my dad's life as part of the club, not to mourn him.

I entered and took a spot by the door, leaning against the wall. These last few days seemed to have crept by, leaving me a little out of sorts. I leave in the morning, and this would be my last night at the club for a while, I hoped to end it between a pair of thighs. As I looked around the room, I spotted the guys who, over the last twenty-plus years, have made up my family. We were born within months of each other—grew up together—even chased and fought over girls together. We'd been the local hotshots in high school and grew into men, the ones most fathers feared would steal their daughters. The six of us were as cocky as they came and caused trouble wherever we went. And yeah, we fucked everything that dared step in our paths. Since as far back as I could remember, we've been referred to as the Sons of Black Hawk.

Smiling, I watched my friends head in my direction. Damn, I love these guys, but I would never admit that aloud because a fight would begin when one of them called me a pussy. Yes, one would, it was a given. We've fought most of our lives, and as I looked at Crusher's face, I could recall that was exactly where he got the scar above his left eyebrow.

We're allowed to give each other shit; it's what brothers do. But that's between us if someone else wanted to give one of us a hard time, well…they better be ready to take us all on.

Crusher's the son of the club's President. One of my best friends who would eventually take over the club when his dad stepped down. I would be one of the Enforcers, and with my dad's death, my spot sits ready and waiting for me to fill it. We each would replace our fathers in whatever position they held when they stepped down. All they waited on was for each of us to find our way, then settle back here to prepare for the position that we have been told over the years we were born to fill.

"Speed, sorry, man, we loved your dad. This club sure is going to miss him," Russ "Crusher" Davis was going to make us a fine Prez when it was his time. Like the rest of us, this club was full of family, and we would do anything necessary to take care of them.

Crusher smacked me on the back and leaned in, giving me the equivalent of a man hug. Then before I knew it, I'm pulled in for man hugs by the rest of my friends, my brothers at heart, and my closest family now—Crusher, Coast, Jag, Flirt, and Devil. No man could ask for better.

"Bro, you head back tomorrow, and we will be following over the next few days," Russ always had to have everything laid out nice and orderly, no detail left to chance. But it was a quality needed in a club president.

"Yeah, I have to get back to the desert. Left my guys a man short. And fuck, that is one place where every body counts, literally." I didn't want to get into the fact I re-upped right before I made the emergency trip home.

"Speed, the dads have been making remarks about as soon as we start trickling our way back here, they want us taking bigger roles in the club to prepare us to take over when they step down. I personally will believe it when I see it, but that's what they keep repeating," Flirt was talking to us, but his eyes were scoping out the room. I shook my head and smacked him on the back to pull his attention to us.

"Man, you can't even look at us for the eye-fucking you're giving the bitches," I knew the statement would get to him, he hadn't earned his name for nothing.

"Oh, I'm looking around because my eyes aren't the only part of me that's going to be fucking before this night is over. I've been checking out the new pieces which have graced the club with their presence. And either I am getting older, or these bitches are getting younger, because, brothers, what is standing in this room is fresh," he glanced over at me and then went right back to looking at the group huddled together across the room.

"You grabbing a piece tonight, Speed, or you going to catch some z's before you head back?" Devil nudged me, and when I looked at him, he burst out laughing.

"Of course, just like you are, huh?" as I raised my eyebrows at him.

"Damn, should we even be joking? I feel so bad about Cutter. Fuck, our dads are supposed to live forever. What the hell!" Jag looked at each of us, frowning. He's the more serious one of our bunch. He's headed back to school to finish his degree, which would benefit the club in more ways than one. As I look at my friend, who, while we were growing up, broke more rules than the rest of us combined, I still couldn't believe the next time I probably saw him, he would be the MC's attorney and more than likely preparing for his eventual spot as VP of the club too.

"Speed, Dad said not to worry. He'd take care of the club issues until you are ready to take your dad's position. They aren't even going to temporarily fill it. The seat stays empty till you come back." Coast smiled at me and nodded his head. Yeah, his dad and mine were the Enforcers in the club. Now it would be left to Coast's dad to cover everything until I came back. One more reason to question why I re-upped. I should be coming home permanently; instead, I'd be shipping back out. Well, it was what it was. No changing things now.

I smiled thinking of what my dad's response to it

would have been. "Kane, shit happens for a reason, you wait long enough, and the path to ride on will change and be all the more enjoyable."

Damn, I was going to miss my old man.

"You boys going to be unsociable tonight? Or you gonna give some of these women something to talk about until you get back for good?" The club's Prez, and Russ's dad, Stroker, said with a smile on his face as he walked toward us.

"Nah, they will definitely be left with plenty to carry them over till we get back. We wouldn't want the new ones to get the wrong impression of the club from you old fuckers." We all laugh at my response, knowing it always got to the older guys even though there had never been such a comment made on any of their performances with the ladies that have come and gone in the club. If anything, it was the exact opposite.

"Hey, why don't you guys give me a few minutes here with Speed, and then you can have him back." Stroker didn't have to say another word, the others walked off, leaving me standing with the Prez.

"Son, you'll always have a place here. You know that, right?" Stroker placed a hand on my shoulder and squeezed. Mitchell Davis, the president of the Black Hawk MC, was referred to as Prez or Stroker, and when I thought back to when we were told how he earned the name Stroker, it always made me smile.

"I know and appreciate it. This is home. I'll be back," I spoke, never turning to face the man. "What's up, Stroker, you thinking I'm not going to want to come back since my dad is gone? This club is my family, always has been."

"Nope, and I know we are your family. I also know you boys talk, just looking toward the future of the club, Speed. Your dad was going to talk with you the next time you came in on leave. We voted, and as you boys start coming back for good, we want to start working you in on the club's business side to prepare you boys for when we turn over the reins. Now with Cutter's spot open, it is there as soon as you want it or are ready to take it over." I heard a small catch in his voice and turned my head to look at Stroker, and for the first time, I noticed the years reflecting on the man's face.

"What will you five do when you step to the side?" I look back to the party. I had doubts they would be able to sit quietly by letting us run shit, but I guess anything's possible.

"We want, when the day comes, to be able to ride for pleasure, relax, and enjoy not having the responsibility of the whole club on our shoulders. Who knows, maybe one of us will take an ol' lady." I'm surprised I didn't get whiplash from the speed I whipped my head around to look at him, and then when I looked at his face, his grin gave away that the statement was a big crock of shit. My brothers and I would be surprised if they ever took ol' ladies. Why, when even at their ages, they didn't hurt for a woman's company?

Sure, our dads are some tough, mean-when-they-need-to-be men, but they had run like the wind over the years if a woman even gave a hint of wanting to tie one of them down. Then again, I see the draw to staying single myself: no one to worry about, coming and going as you please, and the best part—different pussy anytime you want. Though some of the members have ol' ladies and still enjoy a little extra something on the side, most in the club, when they found their other half, that was it for them. Then again, the brothers have found the other half of their souls, so why would they want to chance losing it? Well, at least that was what they said, and it only got said when they were shit-faced because no brother in their right mind would speak of feelings unless he wanted someone to give him shit. I finally focus back on Stroker and my conversation enough to answer.

"I'll do one more tour and come back then," I told him, more to put his mind at ease. With the six of us growing up in the club, our dads raised us to follow the rules at an early age. It's what we know, Black Hawk MC would always be home, no matter how many side trips were taken along the way, we would always end up here.

"You better, you fucking smartass. It still amazes me they let you in with all the artwork on your body. We still laugh about your first day there." He smacked my back and chuckled.

Never would live that shit down.

"I don't know why you guys think that is funnier than shit. I didn't see the fucking humor in them asking me in front of everyone. Hell, I really think some of the guys in my unit believed the shit they were spewing." All I could do was shake my head thinking about the stupidity it took to believe the judge had ordered me to join. All due to the fact I was covered in tats. Dumbasses.

"Maybe it was because you were a scrawny little shit. Cutter and I were glad they put some meat on your ass," Stroker continued to laugh.

I continued to shake my head and roll my eyes, that too was a running joke, because my ass was anything but scrawny at six foot four and two hundred forty pounds of nothing but lean muscle with not an ounce of fat. It started when I hit fifteen and had a growth spurt that shot me past my dad and most of the men in the club. I couldn't complain, hell, that's when the bitches stood and took notice. The night the club celebrated my fifteenth birthday was when I got my first taste of pussy, and I never looked back.

"Kane, what do you want to be done with the busted-up bike?" Prez whispered just for my ears.

"Store it. I want to work on it myself when I get back. That's all I got left of him. You know?" I still couldn't believe my dad wrecked. He was a helluva rider, and I know how he babied his bike, so there wouldn't have been fucking shit wrong with it.

"Anything for you, Speed," he said and started chuckling once more.

"What so fucking funny, now, Prez?"

"Just remembering your first time on a bike. Thought Cutter was going to beat your ass good for getting that ticket?" My Prez was full of himself tonight as he continued laughing.

"Yeah," I joined in the laughter, remembering. I'd barely been sixteen when I got my bike finished. Dad and some of the others had helped me build it. We no sooner got it running and on the road when I was stopped for speeding. "I didn't think he would let me ride after that, but after he had finished bitching at me, he said the cop was a prick, it was my birthday, and the asshole should've let me off with a warning."

Prez squeezed my shoulder, and we went quiet for a moment. I turned back to the party going on around us.

I was going to miss this place.

"Kane, grab a beer and some food, son," Stroker said, calling me by name as he slapped me on the back.

"I will, Prez," I said and watched three new bitches enter through the back, making their way across the room to the bar that was set up. "Fuck me, Stroker. I don't remember them the last time I was home."

"Yeah, got a few new faces around. Daisy invited them. They're new from the strip club. A few of the girls that hang around the club are employed there too. Figured with a few of the visiting members staying, we needed to round up a little extra flesh. Don't need the assholes complaining they weren't treated right in our territory," Stroker spoke as he watched Daisy work her way toward us.

I barely heard Stroker as he continued to talk with me, my attention was on the new girls. First time today I was sorry about having to leave in the morning, definitely would have liked to have gone to the club and watched the one strip down to nothing. But a private show would be all so much better.

"Sure am sorry about Cutter, Speed. Stroker, how

about I take your mind off today for a while?" Daisy said, moving in close enough that Prez and I could see down her cleavage, which was pushing the max in the tight leather vest she sported with nothing under it while she rubbed her hand over Prez's pant-covered cock.

"Can't you see we're talking, dammit," Prez reached out, grabbed her hair, and pulled her up against his body. That was my cue to get the fuck out of the way, because I refused to stand there when he pulled out his cock and Daisy blew him.

Daisy liked it a little rough, and Stroker, well, not that I gave a crap, but he liked giving it a little rough too.

"Sorry, let me make it up—" was all she got out as Prez pushed her to her knees, then looked at me and winked.

Fuck, I wasn't above taking a woman in the middle of the club with my brothers watching, but sue me if I didn't want to watch my Prez's old ass thrusting his hips and sliding his cock in and out of Daisy's mouth.

"Don't let me interrupt. I'm going over to the bar and see if I can't get in on some action of my own."

"Uh…hear ya," Stroker grunted out as his head hit the wall when he threw it back as Daisy's head bobbed and she let out a moan. Oh hell, wasn't going to be eating anything soon, so I headed to the bar with the intention to bury my cock in the little auburn-haired newbie's cunt, the one I saw walk in with the other two women, till the sun came up and I had to leave.

"Going to the bar. See you in the morning before I leave?" I asked, not expecting any of them to be up that early.

"Wouldn't miss seeing you off, Speed." When I turned back at his words, he grabbed Daisy's hair, yanked her head back, then shoved his whole length in her mouth and told her to take it all. Yeah, definitely wasn't going to eat. and sure as fuck hoped I hadn't just guaranteed myself a few nightmares. Wondered sometimes how I survived growing up in the club. Then I smile, because they're the reason we were the men we were today. Wouldn't trade my life for any other.

I leave Stroker getting his rocks off while I go see about acquiring some relief for myself. The women who hang around the club like dick and they're not ashamed to admit it. They get to party on the weekend and let their hair down. Who was I, or anyone else for that matter, to judge them, though there were quite a few who did, then again, the women didn't care and neither did any of the members? Especially me and the brothers, we were the ones who reaped the benefits of their skills. Not going to catch our asses complaining.

Cutter would have liked the turnout. Most people would frown on a party going on after someone died. Not us, it was a party representing how Cutter lived. How we all live. No mourning of death.

As I walked across the room, I noticed Coast and Flirt chatting up the auburn-haired babe. I walked toward them, and she glanced and set her green eyes right on me, then quickly looked back to the men and her friends to who she was currently talking with.

Yep, my relief was getting quenched for the night.

I stopped beside Coast and Flirt, "Hope you don't mind," is what they heard as I bent down and threw my cock's entertainment over my shoulder and turned, taking my prize for the night. I could feel my friend's eyes on my back.

"Asshole, you are lucky we don't kick your ass. Maybe we had some plans for that one. Besides, we got here first, when we're done, you can have a go," Coast said, and I turned back to him. The little thing I'd thrown over my shoulder clued me into what was going on since I caught her off guard with my move, and she started wiggling around on me until I just about dropped her. Me being the prick I am, I slapped her ass.

"Be still," was all I said, and squeezed a handful of soft ass and started to rub her backside, enjoying her squeal after I smacked her ass. The groan that followed when I moved said hand down the back of her thigh and back up, this time going under her tiny skirt. While I was feeling up my prize, I answered Coast.

"Come on, bro, I head back in the morning. You know I can take your ass anyway so really, wasted breath on the threat. Anyway, I should at least get to sample the new goods before I leave," I knew, and they knew she was going with me. My brothers just liked to cause shit when given the opportunity.

"Yeah, Speed, have a goodbye gift. Because when you get back to where you are going, you won't see pussy unless you're into camels," Flirt said, frowning. I knew the frown wasn't for me but more for what he's probably seen. Flirt would also be heading back to his unit in a few days.

I nodded at Flirt, then spoke low enough the others couldn't hear, "It'll be fine, Flirt, we all will, brother."

Flirt turned back to the other women standing there, and I knew that was his way of ending the conversation. I'm sure our demons would follow us when we returned for good. They always do.

My prize for the night decided she had had enough of this and began putting on quite the show, telling her friends they should be helping her. The only thing the other two women did was laugh, then in unison told her to go with it and enjoy herself, before they turned back to Coast and Flirt, and continued their talking, well, their rubbing up against the brothers.

"Hold on, darlin'. Hope you are this fuckin' feisty in bed. I love a challenge," I told my bundle as I turned and headed to one of the extra rooms for the night.

"Uh…you didn't have to just grab me. Asking would have been nice," she actually pinched my ass.

Fuck yeah, the snake wiggling in my arms had a little venom. And damn, I hoped she was willing to share some of it.

"Well, sweet cheeks, this is me asking, so hope you weren't planning to leave, because I need relief, and you are going to give it to me." A moan escaped her as I continued to rub my hand up and down over her ass cheek, working it closer to the heat I could already feel radiating from her pussy.

"You are a Neanderthal; you know that? Maybe if you

had asked instead of just carting me off—" before she finished her statement, she smacked my ass with her little hand. It didn't hurt, it felt more as if a feather hit my ass.

But her feistiness had my cock pressing against my zipper, and I took my hand off her ass to adjust it as I continued to walk. When I placed my hand back on her thigh and ran it under the skirt, I made sure my finger grazed her core. That shut her griping and turned it into another moan. Holy fuck, I was trying to get her back when the move cost me a small portion of my sanity as my fingers slid into her already wet heat, the thong she was wearing wasn't much of a barrier. Which, for me, worked out great, less to remove and the sooner I could sink my cock in.

Damn, I don't remember the rooms being that far from the main room. Every little wiggle of her ass and the soft moans brought me closer to blowing. Something I haven't done in my pants in a long ass time.

Reaching the door, I turned the knob, walked in, then slammed it behind us. No sooner than I set her down, I was on her, and we tumbled to the bed.

Well, hell, maybe the fifteen-year-old boy was still living inside me by the finesse of that move.

I woke, stretched, reached down, rubbed my morning wood, and then flinched. The fucker was sensitive but not that sore. I rolled over with the intention of taking care of the problem one last time before I had to get ready to leave but instead, I hit cool sheets. She was gone. Normally this wouldn't have been an issue, but hell, last night had been one of the best fuck fests, and knowing it'd be a while before I got to enjoy a night like that again with any woman, sucked.

No sense in complaining about it, though, I should actually be thrilled I didn’t have to push her out of the room. I’d hit it, then hit it some more last night and into the early hours of the morning, and now she was gone, it played out just like I liked my fucks to go.

Get in, get out, and then move on to the next. Never a commitment.

Didn't take me long to get my shit together and head to my dad and mine’s place, well, I guess mine now. The place I grew up and, hopefully, the place I would make it back to.

When I heard the guys yell my name from outside, I gathered my duffel, dropped it by the door, and took one last look around, it already felt different without him.

Chapter One

Speed

Fuck, I'm tired; it had been one long ass trip. From the desert to the U.S. had been long enough, but then the last two weeks clearing base was a pain in my ass. Between turning in paperwork, and my physical and psych evaluation, I didn't know if they were going to let me go no matter how many times I told them I was going to be okay. I could deal with death; it wasn't as if I hadn't been around it before. In my book, it is all in how you manage it that makes the man or breaks him.

All they kept focusing on was my unit pinned down and taking casualties until I made a dash for the burned-out truck on the side of the road, killing the bastards hiding behind it. I took fire that day, too, I just happened to get pissed because I was one fucking week from rotating back to the States and gaining freedom of a different kind. I wasn't going to re-up; three tours were enough for anyone. I had been one of the lucky ones, and though I may have killed when necessary, I hadn't been shot or even injured in the ten years I had served—until that last week—the last part of my tour. So yeah, I ran toward the burned-out truck and killed the five insurgents taking cover there. The dumb move cost me two bullets: one in my left shoulder and the other in my right thigh. We'd been in the scout vehicle that day for the convoy, so by the time the rest of the battalion caught up to us, I was bleeding and covered in blood, my own and the rebels. Of the other four soldiers with me, my squad, only one was dead: the newbie we had just picked up that morning, PVT Jones. Besides his death, the other three soldiers that made up my team were just as shot up as I was. The five insurgents, though, laid in a pool of their own blood, good ridden to bad rubbish.

When the doctors were patching me up back at the base camp, they called me one lucky SOB because the bullet that hit my shoulder hit just shy of an artery and only chipped a bone on its way out the other side. They had to dig out the one in my thigh, but a couple of inches to the right on that one, and I wouldn't have one of the women's favored parts of my anatomy. Now *that* I would agree was luck.

I found myself finally cleared. The Colonel signed off on my discharge papers, shook my hand, and told me they hated to lose me. I grabbed what little stuff I had and headed to the parking lot beside the battalion's building. When I reached my bike, I stuffed my belongings in the saddlebags, the rest of it currently on its way back home courtesy of the military, swung my leg over, and straddled the bike. It roared to life, and I took off for the gates and the open road that lay beyond them.

Damn, I couldn't wait. Next permanent stop—*home.*

My ass and legs were sure to cramp when I finally stopped. I'd been on the road for days and couldn't wait to get back to the club. It had been one long ride across the country from Virginia to Washington state.

My nickname, Speed, came from my penchant for flying down the open road and the fact that I had gotten a ticket the first time I'd taken out my bike. I thought I'd never live it down with my dad and the club, my mistake was thinking they had a little more maturity than my friends had. My friends, my brothers, I couldn't wait to see them.

We'd barely had our cuts when we started to leave one by one. It hadn't meant shit our dads were the six military buddies who had founded the Black Hawk MC, we had to bide our time just like every other Prospect. Damn, the closer I got, the more I realized how much I missed the club—my family—more than I would have thought possible.

It would be different this time; I would have to adjust all over again to my dad's absence around the clubhouse. The Marines kept me busy, and I hadn't had to dwell on his death since the day I left after his funeral. Now with each mile that brought me closer, the more Cutter surfaced in my thoughts.

I was raised in the Black Hawk MC, my mother had been a club whore, and when my dad, Harvey "Cutter"

Weston, wouldn't make her his ol' lady, she'd handed me over and walked away, never looking back, I'd been three years old. Rumors traveled through the club that she was bouncing between clubs, trying to find a permanent place; another rumor surfaced that she became an ol' lady at another club. Started using drugs and died of an overdose of heroin a few years before my dad died, the needle still stuck in the vein in her arm when they found her. It had come as no surprise for the members of Black Hawk, she'd been a user when she was with them. It wasn't like I was sad she was gone—couldn't miss something I never had to begin with because even when she was around, she paid no attention to me.

My dad, Cutter, had been an Enforcer in the club. The one who made sure every member followed the rules of Black Hawk. He was also one of the originals.

Looking down at my fuel gauge, I wasn't going to make it all the way in; one more stop was needed. The sun was going down, and I was tired, vowing I would be in my own bed tomorrow night. The next town I came across, I would stop, fill up my tank, grab some food, then stay the night, getting a good night's sleep before making the final leg of my trip and finally reaching my destination. As I passed by the road sign stating food, gas, and lodging at the next exit, I flipped the blinker and made my way down the exit. One more night and a few more hours on the road and I would be at the club.

It'd been a while, and I was ready. At least, I thought so.

The next day, passing the sign that stated Shades Valley, a smile settled on my face. Damn, I was glad to be back. I looked around at the businesses lining the sides of the street and noticed some had changed over while the majority were the same ones as far back as I could remember.

The MC ran some of the businesses in town, like the garage on the corner, Hawks. From the looks of all the cars sitting behind the fence, business was booming, which wasn't a shock because the men that worked there knew their shit. I would have stopped if the gate hadn't been shut, signaling they were closed. Seemed the boys had finished early. As I continued, I passed Inked, the club's tattoo shop, they were closed too, but it was more like they hadn't opened yet for the day.

In the middle of town sat the sheriff's station, city hall, the bank, the post office, and then the B&B grocery. With the edge of town in my sights, I could see the strip club in the distance, and as I drove by, I noticed a few bikes in the parking lot but decided not to stop. I'd reach the club in another ten miles.

I slowed when I reached the turnoff to the club and rode a few minutes up the road until hitting the gate. The Prospect on duty stood and watched as I approached. He didn't look as young as I thought, more like closer to my age. I hadn't been around for a while, so I wasn't going to know most of the Prospects at all.

As I got closer, I watched the guy look me over, his eyes settling on my cut. When he stepped out of the shack, I had been right about him being close to my age, but that was it, the guy was a brute, he had to be six and a half feet tall if he was an inch. His head was shaved, and as I looked him over, I could see the artwork peeking out from the edges of his sleeves. I slowed as I passed, he lifted his chin in acknowledgment, and I rode through the open gate. A minute later, I pulled up to the clubhouse only to be greeted by raised voices and a sheriff's car parked out front.

Killing my bike's engine, I threw my leg over, dismounted the bike, then looked around—yeah, nothing like home.

Chapter Two

Speed

"You're an ass!" was yelled by a pint-sized woman in a deputy's uniform as she faced off with my brother, Crusher. I stepped in and leaned against the doorframe to take in the show. No one had even turned when I walked in, all attention focused on Crusher and the deputy.

Sheriff Lance stood next to the deputy. He'd been the sheriff in these parts since I could remember. The club was lucky to have his backing, he never hassled us. But he expected us to toe the line in return, or at least if we did do something, he didn't want to hear about it.

"Now, sugar, is that nice to say?" Crusher said with a smile plastered on his face. He towered over the woman with his six-three height, but it didn't faze the little thing.

"Don't sugar me, you walking sack of sh—" The

deputy was cut off by the sheriff standing beside her. From my vantage point, I couldn't see his face, but if the shaking of his head was any indication, it maybe wasn't the first time he'd been put in this situation.

"Deputy, don't go there. Christ, I brought you out here so we could get this settled," Sheriff Lance said with a sigh.

"He started it when he passed me on the road. They all," the deputy's arm waved in front to include some of the surrounding brothers, "flew by me. Mr. Davis just happened to be the only one who flipped me off," the deputy finished and crossed her arms over her chest.

"Now wait a damn minute…" Crusher paused, looked up, and before I knew what was happening, he headed in my direction, all but knocking the deputy out of the way.

"Goddammit, Speed, it's good to see you, brother," Crusher yelled out as he wrapped his arms around me and lifted me off the ground. The fucker had always been as strong as an ox because I am anything but a lightweight.

"Didn't want to interrupt the cop powwow. Nice to know nothing's changed while I was away." I hugged Crusher back, and we shook hands. Then the room erupted as the rest of my brothers made it to me.

"What the fuck, Speed. Why didn't you tell us you were coming back?" Stroker said and gave me a man hug.

"Wanted to surprise you guys, Prez."

"Well, that you did, son," the Prez said and stepped away, making room for the others to get in back slaps and handshakes.

As I looked around at the familiar faces of my family, there were several missing, "Where's Devil, Coast, Flirt, and Jag?"

"They're in town. We'll go down to the strip club when they get home and have some fun. Give you a chance to rest and get your stuff settled at your place while we wait for them. You been by the place?" Crusher asked, and all I could do was shake my head in reply. It would be the first time back in the cabin after Cutter's death, and in one instance, I was happy to be back, but in another, I knew it would feel different without him around.

"Jesus, another one. Now the reunion is over, do you think we can get this taken care of before I grow old?" Hell, looked like we'd all forgotten about the sheriff and deputy in the room.

"Ah, sweet cheeks, you feeling neglected?" Crusher turned and spoke to the deputy, and from the fire shooting out of her eyes, I expected him to burn to ashes in front of me.

Just as she opened her mouth to speak again, the sheriff cut her off, "Carly, let's go. Time to let these gentlemen be with their friend." Sheriff Lance started for the door, the deputy following and none too happy by the expression on her face.

"Glad to have you home, Speed. Let's see how long you can be back without getting a ticket," the sheriff laughed and patted me on the back as he walked out the door.

"Never going to live that shit down, am I?" I wasn't asking a question because they hadn't let me forget back then, so why the hell should now be any different? But one could hope.

Most of the men in the room chuckled and then disbursed to do their thing. I was back, and each would catch up with me sooner or later.

"You finished this time, Speed?" Stroker asked.

"Yeah, had enough. It was time to come home," I said, which was the truth for the most part. I'd re-upped before I came back for my dad's funeral, knowing I wouldn't be able to stay around the club with him gone. The Marines kept me busy enough not to think about him every day, but his death still bothered me. Questions plagued my mind at night when it was dark and quiet, and I had time to think about things other than trying to stay alive myself.

Cutter was an excellent rider, yet he skidded off the road in a curve, flipped the guardrail, and hit a formation of rocks, but the bike didn't explode, he'd just been thrown into those same rocks, and even with a helmet on, his neck had been broken on impact. The weather had been clear, nothing in the road that he could have hit to send him spiraling out of control. Not even skid marks from his tires or another vehicle. So the report read the rider had just lost control. Even with everything I had experienced in my life, some things were just not that clear-cut and dry. And with time spent in the desert, I learned to trust my gut—it kept me alive more than once. Now that I was back, I'd have the time to work it out, if I didn't, I know I would never be able to lay Cutter to rest. My dad deserved no less.

"Fuckin' great. It will be nice to have all you boys

home, finally. It's been too long," Stroker said and patted my back.

"Yeah, you say that now. I give it a week with us all here, and we will spend more time in your office than we did when we were teenagers." Crusher was right on that account, the six of us spent a fair share of our youth in that office with our dads yelling at us about respect, loyalty to the club, to our brothers, and most importantly, to ourselves. They taught us the codes to live by, not only as part of an MC but as part of everyday life because each bled into the other. We were taught fear was a great motivator and easy to obtain, but respect and trust were earned, and when you received all of them, the loyalty you would gain from the members would rival no other.

"Yeah, well, you are grown-ass men now, so I'm hopin' not to see you in those chairs other than for business," Stroker said while looking between Crusher and me.

"Don't look at me, Prez, I just got back. Been on the road for damn days. I need a shower, food, and sleep, and not necessarily in that order. After that, well, you never know what kind of trouble one can get into. From what I saw when I walked in, trouble seems to have gotten here a few minutes before me for once," I laughed and raised my brow at Crusher.

"Man, don't start on that. That bitch and I have danced around each other since her ass came into town."

"Yeah, wouldn't have anything to do with her shooting you down all that time either, now would it, son?"

Stroker turned to walk off and stopped to face us once more. "Good to have you back, Speed. Get settled in, get rested, and enjoy the next few days. I expect to see you in Church this week. Don't be late, you know I can't tolerate slackers." He chuckled, turned, and started to walk away, yelling over his shoulder, "Crusher, stay away from the deputy 'til she cools down and bring Speed up to par on things before Church." Stroker turned down the hall and disappeared out of sight.

"Are you under the deputy's skin, man, or what?"

"Or what is a good question. Come on, I'll walk with you to your place. Fill you in. You got stuff on your bike?" Crusher turned toward the door.

"A little, shipping the rest. Didn't want to load the bike down on the trip, so only brought enough to get by. If I need more, I'll go into town and pick some things up," I answered as I followed him out.

We grabbed the bags off my bike and headed around to the back of the clubhouse. A path to the side led to six cabins spread apart that the original six members lived in. Now it would just be me in the one I'd grown up in with Cutter.

"You staying back here with your dad, Crusher?"

"Yeah, but not with Dad. I have the place to myself now. After your dad had died, man, it hit the dads a lot harder than they let on or would admit to. They had a road cut out between these places," he gestured to the cabins we were about to reach, "and the ones on the other side. It runs behind all the places, and they each built them a place back there."

"Damn."

"Feel ya. I didn't know they'd taken it so hard until I got back first. Finished my last stint three years after we were back for your dad's funeral. Did what you did and just showed up one day, going to surprise the old man," he chuckled, "I got the surprise—the place was empty. I opened the door and just stood there. Didn't take long until I heard bikes with the dads on them. Prospect at the gate had called them and said a member from another club was headed up. Told them he didn't recognize me either, so they rode over. Of course, didn't know it was me because I hadn't called. They'd pulled up fully armed. Christ, thank God the fuckers didn't shoot when I walked out the door."

"No shit. They didn't recognize your bike?"

"Nah, sold the old one and picked up another right before I headed back. So after they see me, instead of welcoming his son back, our Prez yells, '*Dumbass, you should have called. You make it through the desert and get shot in your own damn home.*' Then I got welcomed."

"Nice to know they haven't changed in that aspect," I said as we reached my place.

"Nope, not at all. If anything, Cutter's death made them take a good look at their lives. Not that I think they would change anything about how they've lived, it's almost like they feel they should've lived more because you could be gone at any moment."

"Lived more? Seriously, they have lived by their own rules our whole lives. Before that, it had only been their time in service." I didn't understand why our dads would feel that way.

"Not sure why, Speed. I just noticed the difference in them when I came back. That's all."

"So they live out behind the cabins here?"

"Yeah, have their own little compound within the compound." We walked into the living room and set the bags down by the doorway.

I walked to the front windows and cracked them open, the place felt a little stuffy. "Pretty clean for being gone a few years," I said as I looked around.

"The ol' ladies clean the places every week, including yours. They probably know you're back already, but we need to make sure of that," Crusher laughed, "even though they are used to club life, seeing guys getting their dicks sucked, pussy getting eaten out, or club ass getting fucked over the pool table. Nothing prepared Shakes the day she walked in on Devil and Flirt."

Shakes was Dare's ol' lady, he was one of the older men in the club, and Shakes had babysat each of us at one time or another as we'd grown up. She could be considered a surrogate mother to us all. It was another thing the six of us had in common. Born in the same year, months in between, and not one of our mothers had stuck around either, leaving our dads to raise us.

"Oh shit, I guess she walked in on them fucking, but how did she handle it?" Shakes had no problem putting us in our place growing up. If we acted out, she would bust our asses. But she would love on us too. Not that any of us would admit to it, but what little softness we have in us—was because of her. Her old man, Dare, was one of the club's older members, and they were one of the few families that lived in the other spare cabins that sat on club property. They hadn't had any kids of their own, and I didn't know why, because they would have been great parents. Hell, they'd pretty much raised us.

"Man, I was on the porch with Coast at my place. Just so happen that Dad and Cruz were walking up about the time we hear Shakes yell, "what the fuck." Dad and Cruz are running by then, and Coast and I are off the porch sprinting behind them. We hit Flirt's steps as she was stepping out; brother, her eyes were huge. Well, we're thinking fuck, what had she found, but from the bitching going on inside, we at least knew she hadn't found a body. Anyway, Coast and I walk through the door with Cruz behind us while Dad is stuck on the porch, trying to get Shakes settled down. The sight before us was…well, Lindy on a swing that was attached to the rafters across Flirt's ceiling and on her back in it. Devil was standing at her head, and Flirt was between her legs.

"Lindy is yelling to get her down because she is no longer in the mood. Devil's smiling at us, and Flirt is yelling at Lindy to hold still while he gets her the fuck down, all the while there is a humming noise, which ends up belonging to the vibrator that is still on, moving across the floor.

"Coast, Cruz, and I step back out because yeah, we are busting a nut laughing at everything going on because Shakes is yelling at my dad that that is why there are fucking locks on the door. Our boy Flirt seems to have moved into a new field of study by Shakes recount on what happened, which by the way, at this time, Preacher and Flyboy walk up in the middle of her explanation. Seems she walked in, and Devil was holding Lindy's head in place by her hair and fucking her mouth while Lindy's legs were straight up, her heels at Flirt's shoulders as he's rotating a vibrator in her pussy and pounding his meat up Lindy's ass. And on his in strokes, he pulled on the chain attached to the nipple clamps he had on Lindy." When Crusher finished, both of us were adjusting our crotches and laughing because between the floor crawling vibrator and the scene playing before Shakes's eyes, what she was more than likely yelling at was seeing Flirt and Devil bare-assed with their dicks on display.

After we had settled ourselves down, I yawned and sat down on the couch. "I don't remember a Lindy the last time I was home."

"She's been around awhile. Waitresses at the diner during the day and dances at the strip club a couple of nights a week. Bitch has a tight little body, pussy isn't worn the fuck out, and Lindy is up for anything too. Maybe she will be working tonight, and we can sample her goods. Horny thing, too, we might just get her to do us in the back. Club members are the only ones the girls go that extra mile for in the private rooms. Regular patrons only get the dance." Crusher moved toward the door to leave.

"Sounds good to me. I could do with some pussy." Considering I hadn't been laid in a couple of weeks, I could use the release before my balls turned blue. Crusher opened the door and stepped out on the porch.

"I'll come by when I get back from my run into town for Prez. The others should be back, and then we can ride. Grab some grub at the diner, then hit the club."

"Works for me," I said as I stood and walked toward the door. The travel was kicking in, and my body was tired. Crusher must be running on club business, or he would have called Stroker dad instead of Prez.

"Later, Speed," Crusher said and closed the door.

I took one more look around the place, bent for my bags, and headed for my bedroom. Life at home without my dad begins.

Chapter Three

Sami

"Come in!" I yelled to whoever knocked on my door. Never going to get the damn receipts tallied if people didn't quit interrupting me. As the door opened, I set the stack aside, and Tank's body filled the space.

"Hey, Sami, hate to interrupt you, but Perry just finished cooking up the fried chicken for the day. He wanted to know if you'd like some before the Black Hawks start ordering it, and there's nothing left. He knows how you like it and usually takes some home."

My men, that's how I thought of the male employees here at Soft Tails, they looked out for the girls who worked here and me. I was worried when I took over the management of the club about how the males would respond to a woman being in charge. Then again, considering Black

Hawk owned the club, that too could be a great motivator to do your job. Looking back as the big man waited for my answer, I smiled, thinking of the one small girl who walked in and wrapped a group of hardened men around her finger.

"That would be great, Tank. Can you tell Perry to box up a few pieces, and I will grab it when I'm ready to leave?"

"Sure thing, boss," Tank said and turned on his heel to leave.

"And Tank?" I placed a serious look back on my face, at least, I hoped it was serious before he turned back to face me.

"Yeah?"

"Tell Perry no candy in that box either." I watched the big guy's dark brown eyes twinkle because he knew they were busted.

"Ah, Sami, you're no fun. Our girl likes the surprises." Nothing was funnier than when a big man tried to pout.

"Umm…our girl…is not going to have teeth left in her mouth if you men don't stop. And if I can't get you to stop, will you at least pick up some sugar-free stuff? Last time she like to never went to sleep."

"You got it, boss." Tank hurried out after his reply to stop me from scolding him because he knew that I knew they wouldn't stop with the sweets. Why I bothered, I don't know.

Before the door closed behind Tank, three of the girls walked in. There are days I'm surprised I ever got anything done.

"Hey, boss lady," Candie's always called me that since

the first day I started. I met her when I first came to this town. She'd been nice to me, and we had hung out some. When I'd gotten my business degree and landed this job, she'd been thrilled for me. Seemed the last manager had expected freebies on the side from the girls, and if that wasn't enough, the fool thought he could slip a little extra from the till. Ummm…bold move when an MC owned the business you stole from. It hadn't worked out too well for the man, at least, that was what the rumor mill put out.

"Hey, girl, you are early. And I know it can't be that you are trying to impress the boss because I don't swing that way."

"Christ, Sami, if you did, you might have more propositions than you already get with the men that come through this place." I couldn't help but laugh. I may manage a strip club, but the employees here were some of the best people I have met.

"Oh, stop. You make it sound like I have men lined up around the corner."

"Only because you don't pay attention, or you shoot them down when they hit on you," Babs said as she snapped her gum. The only time she's not with a mouth full was when she danced. She'd been trying to quit smoking, and that couldn't be easy in a place full of men every day, half of them puffing away.

"I'm just glad you don't strip, hun. Shit, the rest of us wouldn't make a damn dime." Syn was a petite redhead with green eyes. Her chest alone grabbed men's attention. Toss in her curvy body and flawless skin, and she could make any other woman question her own looks.

I looked down at my breasts and then back up to Syn, "Wouldn't make any money with these babies."

"First off, you have a great set of tits, Sami. And no, I don't go around daydreaming about you like half the yahoos out there." Syn made the gesture over her shoulder, indicating the men out in the bar as if we didn't know who she was talking about. "Besides, you could own a set of these babies for the right price," Syn said as she pushed her breasts together, making Babs, Candie, and I laugh.

"Geez, Syn, you always make me laugh."

"Nothing but the truth, hun."

"Alright, what time is it anyway?" I needed to finish my work so I could head home.

"One," Candie answered as she looked down at her watch.

"Crap, I need to get this stuff finished so I can get home. Mrs. Mayson has a doctor's appointment, and I told her I would come and get Spider so she could go. It's my split day, and I will be back tonight after I get her ready for bed."

"We'll let you get back to work. We gotta go get ready anyway." Candie started toward the door with the other two following behind. When they reached the door, the three yelled, "Later," as the door closed behind them.

I worked on the receipts, counted the money from the night before, and placed it in the safe for deposit. Black Hawk would send someone down each day to take it to the bank. It was supposed to be the manager's duty, but when they hired me, they said they would swing by and do it. My safety being the reason. They didn't want me tagged for carrying around that type of cash. I have to admit, I was thankful. Might be a small town we lived in, but why take a chance?

When I entered the information into the computer, I straightened the desk, grabbed my purse out of the bottom drawer, and got up to leave.

Walking into the kitchen to grab the box Perry had prepared for me, I stopped to talk with him and Bud, the young man who helped Perry out in the evening. We ran a limited menu for the bar patrons: burgers, fries, onion rings, and a variety of cold sandwiches with chips. Once a week, Perry came in early and fried chicken for that night, giving a change-up in the menu. The men who frequented the place had come to enjoy Perry's little change in the items. It never failed that someone would try to get him to add a special item every evening, from wings to pizza. Perry's reply was always the same, "Thought you came to drink and watch the girls, you want shit you get from your wives' or mothers' kitchens, then take your ass to the diner."

"Hey, Perry, thanks for setting aside some chicken for me. Looks like it is starting to get busy out there. I don't know if the girls or your food draws them in." I can't help but tease the man. He was in great shape for sixty-five years old, and he had been a godsend for this place.

"You're welcome, sugar. You know angel face loves my chicken."

"I don't know why you call her angel face, the girl is

like a tornado with legs, and when she does sit still for five minutes, I keep checking on her because it usually means she is contemplating her next move."

"Sami, you need a man before that girl gets to her teens. You're going to need someone to protect her or, at the very least, look out that she doesn't end up in jail. I'm undecided on how that is going to play out."

I had listened to this from Perry almost every day on how I needed a plan of action started so I didn't have to spend my free time beating some random boy off with a bat. Thank God I still had a few years.

As I told Perry bye and headed back toward the front, I waved to everyone as I went by. Frankie was behind the bar, and Bull was watching the floor.

"Darlin', come over here and have a drink with us. I promise we don't bite; if we do, it won't be hard." Stopping by the table closest to the door, I smiled. Roscoe was one of the club's regulars and a member of Black Hawk MC. The man had to be close to Perry's age, but we have had the same banter every time he's in the place and I pass by.

"Ahhh, Roscoe, that won't be the only thing not hard if you keep drinking as you do."

"Darlin', even at my age, that particular organ has no problem getting hard. I am sure all it would take is you to sit that sweet ass on my lap, and it would come to life."

"Roscoe, you do realize you are old enough to be my grandfather, right?"

"You're legal and a woman, age don't mean nothin' as long as you enjoy what's being done to you. And, little girl, doing you would be a pleasure for both of us.

"If'n you need references, ask your girl, Candie, when she comes off the stage. Had her yelling my name last night *and* early this morning." Every Black Hawk member that sat around the table burst out laughing.

"Oh my God, Roscoe, now that was TMI. I'm going home and work on getting rid of that vision. Behave yourself. And, gentlemen, you have a good time, and please don't let him ride his bike back if he keeps drinking."

They each gave a chin lift in agreement, and I turned, leaving them laughing. When I reached the door, Brutus was working and held it open for me and watched while I walked and got in my car, then after I pulled out in the rearview mirror, I saw him close the door.

"Mama!" was yelled as I stepped through the door into Mrs. Mayson's house.

"Hey, baby girl. Have you been good?" I bent down to catch the little body aiming right for me.

"I was…good." I caught her, and she wrapped her little arms around my neck and squeezed.

"She's getting as big as you, Sami," Mrs. Mayson said as she walked out of the kitchen. "And, Ally, did I hear you say you were good today?" Sue Mayson smiled at me and winked. With that, it could mean that yes, she was an angel, which would surprise me more than no, she tied sheets around her and tried to jump off the roof. Sad but true, her tiny frame, her silky black hair to her gold speckled blue eyes yelled little lady, she was anything but.

"Uh huh. I ate all my carrots at lunch." I looked at Sue, whose pursed lips and raised eyebrows told me this was not going to be good, I just hoped it wasn't anything like last week at school when she told her teacher, Mrs. Elderman, that she wasn't growing boobies because then she couldn't play outside without her shirt on.

Ally let me go, looked toward Mrs. Mayson, and then faced me. "I punched Benji in the nose," she said with no apology in her voice, and the expression on her face said she wasn't sorry for doing it.

When I looked up at Sue, she shrugged her shoulders and smiled. Ally never lied, at four she spoke well for her age, was starting to read, and had a stubborn streak that rivaled a grownup's.

"Spider, why did you punch Benji?" Benji was five and went to the same preschool as Ally. They constantly argued. So much so that Mrs. Elderman separated them in class.

"He said I couldn't go to school because I didn't have a daddy," Ally said, and the only hint that what he said hurt her feelings was she sucked her bottom lip in. It was a sure sign she'd been upset.

"You know no matter what people say to you, even if it is ugly, we don't hit them, Ally." She shook her head in agreement but looked none too happy about it. "Go get your bag so we can go home and let Mrs. Mayson get to her errands." Ally left to get her things, and I looked at Sue and sighed. "What am I going to do with her?"

Sue chuckled, "She will grow out of it, Sami. She is rough and tough now, which isn't a bad thing. One day, instead of wanting to do what boys do, she will want to watch the boys doing it."

"Ugh, don't remind me of that. It's not that I don't want her to take up for herself or even be tomboyish, but, Sue, I can't get her in a dress. Last week, she even asked Thelma while we were getting our haircut if she would cut her hair short like a boy's. Now, she has moved on to fighting, what is next?"

"Ally will be fine. Mrs. Elderman wasn't upset, she scolded Benji for saying that to her, but she also said it would depend on what Benji's parents said when she informed them when they picked him up. She didn't seem to think they would make too much of a fuss over it since Benji was wrong in saying that. However, luckily she didn't hit that hard, his nose was red, and his lip swelled a small amount."

"Great." I might have to tell Perry to put his money on jail time for Ally, she seemed to be leaning in that direction.

"The reason that all happened was that in a few weeks, they have a day where the dads come to the school and do crafts and eat lunch with the kids. That was when Benji said she couldn't come that day because she didn't have a daddy."

"Well, I can't run out and buy her a daddy. We've had the talk, she knows why she doesn't have a daddy. At least as close to the talk as you can have with a four-year-old. She knows he is gone. She knows he didn't know about her when he left. I explained the best I could to her when she asked why she didn't have one," I whispered, not wanting for Ally to hear any of our conversation.

"Oh, honey, there are men out there who don't have a problem raising other men's kids as their own. But if you don't go out, you won't find one. And don't say you are around men all day." She smiled.

Knowing she was right and actually doing something about it were two different things. Between Ally and my job, there wasn't much time for socializing. And when I was off, it was time to catch up on chores and spend extra time with Ally.

When Ally walked back in dragging her bag, nothing else was said. She hugged Sue goodbye, and I told Sue we would see her later. Sue would come over to my house next door and stay with Ally while I went back to the club.

"Come on, baby girl, let's get you cleaned up, and your pj's on before Mrs. Mayson gets here." Ally finished her dinner while I straightened up the kitchen.

"Can I see what candy Perry sent me now?" She pushed her plate away and smiled at me. I hadn't said a word to her about the chicken being Perry's, and she still knew. She also knew those men wouldn't forget to put something in the box either.

"There wasn't any candy in the box, baby girl." I watched her brow furrow, it would be the first time she didn't get some kind of candy from Perry or one of the guys. Tank must've told Perry what I said, so yes, they went in another direction. I was undecided about which would be worse where they were concerned. "But…" I paused, dragging it out.

"But what, Mama?"

"No candy, but they sent you a cupcake." And I had to smile as she bounced in her seat when I picked up the small box and set it down in front of her.

"Yay! My favorite," as she dived into her chocolate cupcake with chocolate icing from Claire's Bakery in town. Which meant one of the guys would have had to run there and back to pick it up. They spoiled the girl rotten.

"Finish that, and then you can get in the bath."

"'K," she said around the cupcake.

Ten minutes later, Ally was in the bathtub, and I was redressing in work clothes out of the sweats I'd put on to lounge around the house comfortably.

When the doorbell rang, we were just headed down the steps. I was ready for work, and Ally was ready for a little TV before bed. Pulling the door open for Sue, I quickly stepped back before Carly barreled in instead of Sue.

"Ugh, I have had a shitty day, do you have any wine, beer, or poison?" My friend headed straight down the hall toward the kitchen, and as she passed Ally, she yelled, "Hey, short stuff."

"You said a bad word, Aunt Carly," Ally yelled back.

"Yeah, yeah, what are you, kid, the word police?" Ally giggled, and Carly opened the refrigerator, then I heard the top pop on a beer. As she walked into the room where I was now sitting on the couch with Ally, she plopped in the chair across from us and sighed.

"So, a bad day on the criminal front?" And that was all

it took for my closest friend to start.

"I had another run-in with Mr. I Look Good, and every woman should want to have a piece of me." She took a long pull from her beer.

"What did he do now? And remember little ears are in the room, she knows way too much now as it is," I reminded Carly about Ally before she got wrapped up telling her story and forgot Ally was in the room.

"Oh, yeah, don't want to further her education. Though she should learn that some men are not worthy of an ounce of our time. What the…" Carly paused, probably to think of a word that wouldn't be so bad if repeated by Ally, "jerk did was ride by me today with his friends, and as they passed, he flips me off. I radio into Mabel at dispatch that I was going to follow them, and then the sheriff comes on and tells me to head back to the station and pick him up, he went with me. We said we needed to get whatever was going on with Mr. My Personal Pain in the Butt and me because he was tired of listening to the bitching about their club. Can I help it if the man provokes me at every opportunity? He has since I got the job of deputy last year. What the effing hell, should I just let them run over me because they are big bad bikers?" she huffed.

"Well, umm…is there something going on with you and him?" I inwardly cringed because that was going to set her off. We'd grown up in a club and moved to Black Hawk territory at my dad's request, the only reason given was there was stuff going on in the club that needed to be taken care of, and he didn't want to have to worry about us being caught up in the middle and used against him. I hadn't wanted to up and move, but my father was a no-argument type of man. And being raised in a club and knowing that sending us into another club area meant what was going on had to be serious. I had to admit, though, Carly had it rougher, but she never would tell me everything that had gone on in her house. As I watched Carly rub the label on the bottle, I knew she was thinking of that time. Growing up in the Haven MC hadn't been bad, we were a family. Even when we'd walk into the clubhouse and catch one of the men getting sucked off, we either continued through as though nothing was going on or we turned around and left. It was part of life in the MC, and if we did walk in on things we shouldn't have, it was likely because we weren't supposed to be there.

"No, there is nothing going on. You know I don't want to get swallowed up by a club again. My dad was bad enough before my mom died, the drugs and booze, then the fighting because they were so messed up. After was too much. He changed from a protective dad to he didn't care if I had lunch money or even if I went to school. From the time I was fourteen, he told me every day that he couldn't wait until I was gone or someone else's burden. You had and have a great dad." She smiled for the first time since she entered.

"I don't have a daddy," Ally said with her eyes still on the TV. I looked over at her and then at Carly. Evidently, my baby was still thinking about earlier today with Benji. I didn't want to get into this with having to go to work in just a few, and I didn't want to explain to Carly what brought this on. But Carly was close to Ally, and I knew she wouldn't let it go.

"Spider, you don't need one, you have a ton of men who care about you." Carly raised her eyebrow at me, signaling 'what the fuck'. I watched Ally's face as she turned toward Carly.

"Perry sent me a cupcake, and I punched Benji in the nose." And as quickly as she started, she stopped and turned back to the TV. And Carly laughed.

"Okay then, would you like to tell me what that was about?" she asked me.

I filled Carly in on Benji and the nose, along with Perry's cupcake instead of candy. When I finished, the doorbell rang again, and I looked at my watch. Yep, time to go to the club, and Sue should be on the other side of the door.

As I opened the door and Sue came in, Carly went to the kitchen and threw her bottle away.

"I shouldn't be past eleven, Sue. I'm not closing tonight."

"Okay, honey. I'll be here whenever you get home. Carly, good to see you."

"You too, Sue. I'm going to head home and yell if you need anything while Sami is gone. Later, short stuff." And as fast as she'd entered earlier, Carly was out the door.

Sue was sitting with Ally on the couch when I walked back in with my bag and keys in hand.

"Give me a hug, baby girl," and Ally stood on the

couch to reach so she could wrap her arms around my neck, “love you, baby, and be good for Mrs. Mayson.”

“Love you too, Mama,” she said and flopped back down on the couch.

“Thanks, Sue, see you in a few.” I reached the door, opened it, and before I closed it behind me, Ally’s voice rang out.

“Mama, can you bring me home a daddy?” And I heard Sue’s chuckle as the door clicked shut.

“Yeah, let me get right on that,” I muttered to myself as I got into my car. Seemed my daughter wasn’t ready to move past the daddy issue.

Yay me!

Chapter Four

Speed

When my eyes snapped open, it took me a few minutes to realize where I was. *Home.* It'd been a while. I stretched and then sat on the side of the bed, taking in the room. It had to have been Shakes. She had all Cutters things boxed and furniture switched out in the main bedroom with mine from the bedroom I'd used up until I'd left for the service. The woman was a sweetheart. She'd even labeled what was in the boxes in the other room: clothes, shoes, personal items, and papers.

Yeah, I'd get to those soon. Just not today.

I stood and headed to the bathroom. Sleep had come first after Crusher left. Now it was time for the shower, then a look around the place.

With two of the s's done, I searched for my clothes.

The third 's' I decided to skip. Being out of the military, it would be a trial to see how long it would take for the stubble to get on my nerves.

Stepping out the back door of the cabin, I looked around, the place had been well taken care of while I was gone. More of Shakes work, I'm sure. I headed across the grass, unsure if I was ready for this next step, as I stuck the key in the lock and opened the door on the side of the garage. When I flipped the light switch, the open space lit brightly. Scanning the space, I overlooked the benches holding every tool you would need to work on bikes, even spare parts that lined the shelves. Nope, my focus settled on the tarp off to one side.

Reaching it, I grabbed the end and pulled the tarp back, revealing the mangled bike beneath. As I ran my hand over the dented, scarred, and broken metal, I thought of my dad and, for the first time ever, wondered what had gone through his mind in those last seconds before he crashed. My plans were to strip the bike down and start piecing it back together from scratch. It was my last tie to him, and I planned to keep it as long as I could, even if it was only the rebuilt model.

Harvey Weston had been a great dad. Of course, he made mistakes along the way, but who doesn't, but he also admitted to them. Not often mind you, but some. Mistakes made still didn't keep him from being a great dad.

Clarice, my mother, I use the term lightly, was a club whore. She'd grown up in Shades Valley, from what I had been told about her, lost her parents at an early age, and ended up being raised by an aging grandmother, who died, leaving her without family at the age of eighteen. She worked at the grocery store in town, lived in the local trailer park, and spent weekends at the club partying. That was where my dad came into the picture, along with the other men in the club. He just happened to be the one she set her eyes on.

I didn't remember much about her, and I never asked. What I learned was said to me by Cutter when I reached horny teenager status.

"Kane, I noticed you've been sniffing around a few girls in your class. Boy, have you got your dick wet in any of them yet?"

"No, sir."

"Here," he shoved a box of condoms at me, "before you run out, tell me, and I'll get you more."

"Yes, sir."

"Don't stick your dick in without the damn raincoat. You don't know what any bitch could be planning. And always use your own."

"What for? A condom is a condom."

"Goddamn, Kane, no, it isn't. But, son, I don't want what happened to me and a few others to happen to you."

Cutter proceeded that day in telling me how Clarice had evidently done alterations to a stash of condoms. A reserve kept by Cutter in the room he used at the clubhouse. She ended up pregnant, and it was too late when she'd let it slip during one of their frequent arguments that she planned it because she wanted to be his ol' lady. Unfortunately, Cutter hadn't been the only one in his stash, and five other women who frequented the club ended up pregnant. And over a period of months to follow, the sons of Black Hawk were born.

I rubbed the back of my neck, and the heat was there just like it was that day. I didn't want to have 'the talk' with my dad any more than most young boys would like to. Even thinking back didn't make the conversation any less embarrassing, but I learned a lot from that talk. And lived by that knowledge too. Not once have I fucked without protection, no matter what the woman said, and I damn sure carry my own condoms. No wetsuit, no diving in the pussy pool for my cock.

"Yo, he's in the garage." I stepped back from the bike and saw the smirk on Devil's face as he pushed off the doorframe and walked toward me.

"How long your ass been standing there?" Christ, I hadn't even heard him approach the door.

His expression changed as the smirk left, and his eyebrows creased, "Just a minute or two, you were pretty engrossed with the bike there." Devil stopped in front of me, looked at the bike, grasped my hand, pulled me into a hug, then stepped back.

"Fuckin' great to see you, brother."

"You too, Devil."

"Bike's fairly fucked up. What are you thinking of doing with it?"

"Rebuild it." More boots were heard, and in walked the rest of the guys.

"Damn good to see you, Speed." Jag walked up, giving

me a man hug and slap on the back, followed by Flirt and Coast.

"What are you doing out here? I thought we'd catch your ass still sleeping." Crusher was the last to step in.

"Checking things out. I did sleep. The place looks good. I was expecting to have to do some work around here. Instead, it looks like all I have to do is grab groceries for the place. If the truck starts up." I glanced over to the black SUV Cutter, and I drove around in during the winter or if we needed it to pick up something that couldn't be carried on a bike.

"It's been taken care of while you were gone. Started and drove enough just to keep it going." Jag shrugged like it wasn't a big deal.

"As far as the place being taken care of, that was Shakes and a few other ol' ladies. By the way, Dare came into the clubhouse before we headed this way and said the women heard you were back; they been cooking all day. So you, my man, will get hit with a shit ton of food." Coast laughed.

"I ain't going to complain, my ass is hungry, and home-cooked food works for me." No way I would turn down a home-cooked meal after eating mess hall food or MREs out on patrol.

"Not arguing. Those women can cook." Flirt rubbed his belly as he spoke. How he stayed fit, I didn't know how. He could put the food away. But, then again, I probably didn't want to know how he did.

We walked out of the garage, and I locked the door.

When I turned around, a truck was pulling up, and we watched Dare step out of the driver's side as Shakes jumped down from the passenger side. As I watched her, she looked at us and then zoned in on me, then the smile spread across her face.

"Got food the women cooked," Dare said as he walked up and clasped hands with me. That was all he got out before Shakes moved him out of the way and latched onto me. I wrapped my arms around her and picked her up, she'd always been a little thing.

"All my boys are home," was said, followed by sobs. I hated tears on women. I never knew what to do about them.

"Oh, for fuck's sake, woman. They are grown-ass men now. They have been, and why are you crying." I sat Shakes back down on her feet and wiped at her tears as we waited for her to pull herself together. Finally, she settled, and the woman who had mothered us was back in place.

"It wasn't the same without them here together. Been a long time. Now this place feels right." She stared up at Dare.

Dare shook his head at her, "You don't get all emotional and shit when I come home."

"Oh stop. You don't go anywhere other than to the clubhouse or the strip club. And yeah, before you start, I know, I know. You only go down there to hang out with the guys. It isn't like you look at the young girls dancing. Please." Shakes rolled her eyes.

"Woman, you did not roll your eyes at me. I have never given you a reason to think I fucked another woman.

What the hell." We stood quietly and watched them go back and forth. From the look on the other's faces, they, too, were trying to bite back their laughter. Even though some of the brothers may stray a few times, Dare was never one of them. Shakes and he had been together for a lot of years.

"Dare, I ain't complaining or insinuating that you go down to the club to pick up one of those young bodies. Why would I, when, sweetie, I'm the one who benefits from you watching them shake their stuff." Dare's eyes changed as he looked at her, then he grabbed her up, and she wrapped her legs around his waist. I coughed, and the others groaned. Dare looked over her shoulder at us and winked.

"Get the food out of the truck. I need to take my woman home."

He didn't have to say it twice. We unloaded the boxes, and he had Shakes in the vehicle and was pulling away before we stepped back into my place.

"Let's eat, I'm starved, and then we can head out to the club." My stomach growled just as I spoke. The women had definitely outdone themselves. They even packed drinks to go along with the food, and in a separate box were groceries. I guess I wouldn't have to run out to the store for a couple more days.

"How's it feel to be home, Speed?" Crusher said, handing over a plate.

I looked at each of the men as we stood in my kitchen, setting out the food and working together doing it. It'd been a long time since we'd been together like this. I turned toward Crusher to answer.

"Never better, brother. Never better," as I loaded down my plate.

With our stomachs overloaded, the walk back to the clubhouse, where our bikes sat in the parking area in front, was much needed. I hadn't realized how hungry I had actually been.

The ride to Soft Tails was short but one of the best rides I'd been on in quite a long time. Nothing beat the six of us riding together; it'd been a while.

"Let's grab that table over in the corner, and then we can see about getting one of the girls to bring us some drinks," Crusher was already headed in that direction as he yelled over his shoulder.

"Place is doing good business, it seems?" The place was packed, not just with the brothers from the club. I never remembered it being this busy, even when we opened it a few years ago.

"Damn, Syn hugs that pole like it's going to get away from her." I looked up at Flirt's words to see a petite redheaded woman with her legs wrapped around the pole and her back arched flat to the pole while she hung upside down. Then in slow motion, she grabbed the pole with her hands and released her legs to flip them over and land on her feet on the stage. When she dropped to her knees and crawled to the end of the stage, the men in front got louder. I figured it had everything to do with how her tits were hanging on to the top, her nipples the only thing keeping them contained.

"Can I get you, boys, something?" was said just as a hand ran over my shoulder. At the question and touch, I looked up to see a short-haired blond with brown eyes looking at me while she spoke.

"Yeah, bring us beers all around. When are you dancing, sugar?" Flirt asked while his hand landed on her ass, rubbed down, then back up under her short black skirt.

"You got it. And I'm dancing in a bit. So who's the new hottie," she said, presumably to me since she smiled and winked, and that hand of hers continued to rub over my shoulder.

"Speed, this here's Lindy," Flirt jerked his head in my direction, "now can you take your ass and go get our beers." Okay, Flirt definitely had the no argue voice going on because the bitch turned in a huff and headed to the bar.

"Dude, what's up with that? She ain't under your command, at least right now." Devil looked pointedly at Flirt.

"Hey, is she your property, Flirt? Going to claim her?" I watched the smirk as it formed on Flirt's face.

"No way, I'm thirsty, and if we let her stand there touching you, we wouldn't have gotten our beer until after she'd blown you." The others chuckled, and I looked at each brother until I returned to Flirt.

"Happen often with her, does it?" But still felt like I missed something.

"You haven't said nothing to him, Crusher?"

"If you're talking about you and Devil having her at your place and Shakes walking in, well yeah. What's the big deal? You upset everyone knows about how you like to dish it out before getting off, don't sound like you, brother?"

"Nope, I got no problem sharing—as long as it goes my way." Then Flirt took the hand he had up her skirt and wiped it with a napkin he grabbed off Lindy's tray when she stepped to the table with our beers. "But as she was touching and talking to you, her pussy was clenching, and my hand was getting moist, I figured she was a minute away from blowing or riding you. Isn't that right, Lindy girl?" She leaned over me to set the bottle down in front of me, and I took that opportunity to look at the tits pressed to my forearm and perfectly in view with her nipples hard and trying the confines of her shirt.

"You know it," she said to Flirt, but her eyes were on me, "I like to do my part in welcoming the new guys." Her tongue came out to moisten her lips. Yeah, I could picture them wrapped around my cock as I held her head and fucked her mouth. She had lips guys like to call fuck-able: big and plump, made to take a beating. Good cushion for her teeth and the guy's dick.

"Brother, take her to the back room and let Lindy show you what she can do. She seems a little hot for you, brother." Crusher smiled at me. I didn't lie about the girl being a horny thing, that's for sure, as she placed her hand on my crotch and ran it back and forth.

"Sugar, you don't need to check the size. I got more than enough for you to handle."

There was a throat clearing, "That may be, but she will have to find that out later."

Lindy moved her hand, and I turned my head to see who belonged to that voice, and the woman in front of me, shooting daggers in Lindy's direction, was fine.

"Sure thing," Lindy said as she walked away from the table.

"Sorry, Sami—"

I cut Jag off with a raised hand, "Darlin', I'm not really worried about her finding out what I'm packing, but now, you, I could seriously—" Crusher stopped me from finishing my sentence, and the woman they called Sami had me pinned down with dagger shooting from her eyes.

"Um…brother, meet the manager Dad hired to run Soft Tail for the club. Sami, this here is Speed. Speed, meet Sami." I looked at Crusher, then looked at the other brothers to see if they were just playing me, and each one tried to bite back their laughter. Fuckers.

"What, come on, tell me you are dancing later. I want to move up closer when you get on stage. Want to see that fine ass and ti—"

"Brother, Crusher was telling the truth. Sami here runs the place."

"You're shittin' me?" I replied to Coast, but I didn't need them to answer as she stomped her feet, mumbled under her breath, and walked away. Great damn first impression. "Stuff sure has changed," I voiced as I watched her move to the bar and speak to the bartender.

"Yo, don't even think about going there, brother. She's turned everyone down that has tried to get close enough to tap it." Devil smacked Flirt on the back when he spoke.

"Tried to go there, did you, man?" Flirt turned from watching the stage and cocked his eyebrow at me.

"If I had tried to get in those panties, do you really think she'd have turned me down?" Then he turned back to the stage—cocky bastard.

"Seriously, Speed, I told you the dads changed after Cutter's death. I came back, and they had those cabins built for themselves. They spent the time we were away from here, cleaning up the operations." Crusher stopped to take a swig of his beer.

"Clean it up. What the hell," my response came from the fact we six had planned to go legit once we took over. I was just shocked it was already in the works.

"They cut the ties last year with our last customer across the border. I'm sure Stroker will fill you in at Church this week." They had been busy while we were gone. Now staying away so long made me feel a little like shit. I don't know about the others, but I'd have liked to have been here to help with it all.

"I can tell by your face you feel the same way we all did when we started to come back. Feel like you should have been here, huh?" Coast was always spot on in his observations, probably the reason he'd done so well as part of the Delta Force.

"What made them go that route?" The thought briefly ran through my mind that no way in hell was the old men going soft. And I do mean briefly.

"Like Jag said. Prez will fill you in at Church with

everything we got going on. But, brother, you will still be in the dark about why. Never gave a reason for it other than he said it was done." Crusher shrugged and tipped his beer.

"Guess I will wait for Church."

I tipped my beer toward the others, and they did the same. Then we all faced the stage when the music started again and watched the blond, curvy stripper begin her routine.

Chapter Five

Sami

I'd gotten back to the club, and it had been a full house tonight. Tank was at the door when I came in, got his usual chin lift in acknowledgment because his eyes were keeping watch. I was not sure if his awareness of his job was why he hadn't spoken or if it was his way to avoid me getting on him for the cupcake sent to Spider. He might have been a big man ,but he was still a man. Avoid all confrontations with a woman if you can get by with it. News for him. I'd just wait and pounce his ass when he least expected it.

My job was trying on a good day, but I loved it. The people I worked for and worked with were great. It hadn't been that way to start; it took my first six months to whip it into shape. And as long as my bosses were happy, that's pretty much all I cared about.

Checked the bar as I'd passed through, checked the kitchen to make sure Perry didn't need any extra help, then made my way to my office, where I dropped my purse.

I'd just stepped out to go make sure all the girls had shown up to work when I spotted Lindy at the table in the corner. When I'd seen her lean over on the one biker's arm, flashing her tits wasn't what pissed me off. Nope, it was the hand she ran across his crotch. I ran this place, I'm not naïve to anything that goes on, but not on my damn floor. Take it to the back if you want to earn a good tip. Though I shouldn't have been pissed, I was just tired, and working the double day always made me feel guilty leaving Ally.

When I reached the table, all eyes had been on Lindy, so I'd cleared my throat before I'd spoken, gaining everyone's attention. Bikers didn't scare me, I'd wanted Lindy to get back to work, and as her eyes met mine, she'd known she was busted. However, the biker she'd been groping caught me off guard. He'd turned, looked up at me, and his blue eyes stopped any other words from leaving my mouth. So much so, I didn't even hear but half of what he'd said, something about ass before he was cut off by Russ Davis, one of the bikers he was with, and my main boss's son who went by Crusher. Lucky day for me. Not. I continued to just stare at the man until they introduced me, and he didn't believe I ran this place. Were they shittin' him? Really?

Though still, I stood there, only now pissed that he thought I wasn't capable. But what pissed me off more and if you could have two emotions fighting each other for dominance, I'd felt like my heart had dropped to my stomach. Because the eyes that looked back at me were my daughter's eyes.

Well, she had asked me to bring her home a daddy. Yeah, that ran through my mind, go figure. So then my best option had been to stomp off and berate myself while I'd done it.

Hadn't made it in to check if all the girls showed up. Nope, I'm a grown-ass woman and a mother, for God's sake. Yet, into my office I went after I stopped off to tell Stem where I would be.

Once in my office, I'd immediately went to the cabinet on the wall and opened the doors to the monitors that revealed everything going on in the club, from the kitchen, the bar, the hallway leading to the dressing room the girls used to the bathrooms. I could even see my office door on the screens. If I flipped screens, I could see the front and back of Soft Tails. Everything in view. The only privacy to be had was in the bathrooms, inside the actual dressing room, and the private lap dance rooms, which sat at the end of the hall. My focus zoomed to the table in the corner where the men watched the girls, spoke amongst themselves, and enjoyed each other's company. They laughed, slapped one another, flirted with the girls, and drank. All the while, I watched the one they called Speed. Granted, he hadn't thought me capable of being the manager, which made me mad. But what I realized more was the hurt that there hadn't even been a flicker of recognition on his part—when I've dreamt of him and our night together every night for almost the last five and a half years.

What the hell am I doing, I asked myself. My only answer his damn eyes, the dark blue with gold speckled in their depths. That's what I saw when we looked at each other across the room. His short black hair and those eyes, but oh, I could picture him with long locks, just enough to run my hands through. The man didn't even tell me his name, but I thought I heard the other two call him Speed. I know MCs, and it makes me wonder how he'd earned that road name. I was ready to ask him when we entered the room, but before I could say anything he lowered me to my feet, and his lips met mine. Holy hell, his lips were hard against mine as he devoured my mouth.

By the time he ran his tongue across the seam of my lips, I was lost in him and opened my lips, giving him just enough space to slip his tongue in, which he did, diving in full force.

I thought I was prepared for what was going to happen when I showed up at the Black Hawk MC. New in town, sticking to what I know, how bad could that be, so when a couple of the girls I'd met invited me, I didn't hesitate to accept. Especially when the men from the club frequented the diner I worked at, not to mention a few of the women I'd met that worked at the strip club the MC owned.

He literally had thrown me over his shoulder, and I had been momentarily caught off guard. Once my senses came back, I tried to make him put me down, but of course, all that did was lead to him smacking my ass, then his light rubbing had me wet and moaning. I'd only been with one man before, or boy since I had been in high school when we'd slept together. Not that I was much older than eighteen, I'd only graduated that past year.

Yep, pretty sure the man thought I was one of those women who got off coming to the clubs just to say she slept with a biker. Especially the way I'd reacted to his touch. Nope not me, but I didn't think he would believe me if I told him it was something about him, how could I get him to understand when I couldn't explain it to myself other than at the first look into his eyes I was caught.

Sure, that wouldn't sound crazy at all. His lips left mine and began a trail down my neck, across my collarbone, and back up the other side until he reached my earlobe, sucking it into his mouth. My eyes rolled back in my head, and the time to think was over.

"Strip," he stated with a gruff voice.

"What?" I swear, at that point, he sucked my brain cells through my earlobe.

"Strip, I can't wait to be deep in your pussy, so if you want to salvage your little skirt and thong you have on, now would be the time."

Screw it, let him think what he wanted, I stepped back, looked into his eyes, and began removing my clothing one piece at a time. When the last piece of my clothing hit the floor, I stood before him naked, and I should have felt exposed or nervous, but the feelings didn't come. His eyes started at my feet, and as his eyes lifted, it was as if he physically touched me. I felt the warmth work its way up my body. His eyes met mine, and I know I should have been scared by what was reflected in his—instead, the desire sent a shiver of want to my core.

"Goddamn, I was in a rush to be inside you, now looking at you naked makes me want to take my time and not leave any spot untasted or untouched."

I couldn't talk, I only continued to stare at him.

"Ah, don't worry, baby, you aren't going to need to talk. You're only going to feel with all the things I want to do to you." He stepped toward me, never breaking eye contact with me.

I'd never felt like that. My first time had been in the park in the grass, and the boy had lasted all of five minutes. And looking at this man, I could honestly say my first time was with a boy. Because by the promise that showed in this man's eyes, I didn't have to be experienced to know he would forever change the way I thought sex should be.

I blinked first, and in the millisecond it took, the control he was holding over his body snapped, and he was on me.

Compared to him, I was so inexperienced, but inside me, the fire from his touch, the heat in his lips as he kissed my lips down to my chin, my neck, my collarbone, to settle on my breast, left me burning. And when he sucked, then bit down on my peaked nipple, and his tongue laved the sting away, my pussy moistened and spasmed with the want of what he was offering me.

I placed my hands on the sides of his t-shirt, untucking it from his pants, pushing it up, and sliding my hands with it to get my first real feel of his warm and inviting skin. As my hands reached his nipples and my fingernails raked over each, he pulled away, the cool air of the room hitting my breast instantly made me miss his warm mouth.

His shirt was pulled over his head and tossed to the side, and as his hands undid his pants, I got my first look at his cock as it was freed: long, thick with the veins noticeable from his arousal.

The only thought I could process was that he is huge—everywhere.

Then he engulfed me.

Back was the man that had grabbed me out in the club. Hands roamed my body, lips trailed over every inch of my skin, coming back to capture my mouth. His tongue pushed in, exploring every crevice. All I could do was wrap my arms around him and hold on.

The kiss broke, and he reached to the side, grabbed a condom, and pushed up onto his knees. I didn't even see him place them on the bed in the first place, a sign my attention had been elsewhere.

"First time goin' to be hard and fast, darlin', I'd say the next time might be slow but don't count on it," he said while ripping open one of the foil packets and rolling it down his length.

"First time?" I'd only focused on those two words as he'd spoken to me.

"Fuck yeah, been a while for me, so one time in that pretty pink pussy ain't going to be enough."

I opened my mouth to respond as he leaned over me, one hand placed on the bed beside my head while the other lined his cock with my entrance. As the head made contact with my pussy, a shiver of anticipation ran through me.

"So wet and warm." His eyes were on mine as the head of his cock moved up and down, spreading the lips of my pussy, gathering the juices to allow him to slide in. I moved my hips up and down, following his movements, wanting him to take me.

"Stop teasing," I'd found my voice.

His grin, followed by the pressure at my opening, had me grinning back at him. I was getting my way.

"Ah, darlin', you're gonna get what that little pussy wants, and then so—" His words cut off as he pushed in and groaned. "Goddamn, you're tight, gonna blow before I get there."

He worked his cock in and out, sliding deeper with each thrust in till his pelvic bone hit my clit, and I moaned, the nub hard and sensitive to the touch. He filled me, and I stretched around him to just this side of pain. Holding still, his breathing picked up, and when I focused back on him, he was gritting his teeth, then I felt his body shake from the exertion he was putting forth not to move while I adjusted to his size, but I needed him to.

"Can you move, please?" My words came out breathlessly. The sign he must have been waiting for because he pulled all the way out and slammed back in, picking up speed with each pump.

My hips pushed up to meet his. With every push in, his pelvis rubbed against my clit. The slap of skin hitting skin and our breaths were the only sound in the room until the hands holding some of his weight off me buckled, and he pushed them under me, grabbing my shoulders with his hands. He was holding me in place while his hips sped up, then the sound of the headboard hitting the wall joined the noises in the room as he pounded into me.

I felt the pressure build, the orgasm hitting me and racking my body so hard it stole my breath. He rode the tremors, and when my body started to settle, he raised up and grabbed my hips, pulling me with him. With every thrust in, his cock bottomed out, one, two, three more, and he collapsed back on me, pulling me tight into his body while he rode out his own release.

The knock on the door made me jump as it opened, and Tank stuck his head in.

"You okay, heard moaning as I passed by. Thought I better check." Great, the man comes back, and now I go from dreaming at night to daydreaming about him. Wonderful, and he didn't even remember my face.

"Yeah, it was probably a yawn you heard. Tired." Was as good an excuse as any.

"Go home, we're almost emptied out. We got this, boss lady. Get some sleep." This was why my guys were great. I could leave and know the place would be in good hands and closed down right.

"I think I will, thanks, Tank."

"Sure thing, Sami." The door closed, and I rose out of my chair, doing what I needed to before heading home. If I worked hard not to think of the man, maybe, just maybe, I would be able to sleep without him entering my dreams.

Then again, why should tonight be any different?

Chapter Six

Speed

"Anyone wanna fill me in on what's going on around here? Stroker hired a woman to manage Soft Tails, and the club is legit? Next, you're gonna tell me we have fuckin' tea parties at the club." Not that having a woman run the club was wrong, it was more that I was caught off guard when I turned and saw her, using the grumpiness to cover the shock.

Crusher leaned forward and placed his elbows on the table, "Well, you met Sami. Evidently, when they started down the legal road, they thought the strip club needed a new look." Before Crusher could go on, Coast leaned in.

"And cleaned up and out. The place was shit when I came through on leave a couple of years back. Strippers were using the product, which I'm not against, but the girls were strung the fuck out, even on stage. As far as dipping your stick, hell, I didn't even let them put their mouth on me. Fucking rubbers ain't made of that thick of material. Even if it's free pussy, there should be standards. Prez had had enough. He sent Dad to lay the law down on them, a little reminder that though not part of Black Hawk, they were working for the MC by dancing in our club."

"Damn." It had to have been bad, most people didn't like to get on the bad side of an MC, regardless of the circumstances. Clubs had permanently gotten rid of offenders who tried to muscle in on their area or push against them and interfere in their business.

"Yeah, but to make it short, they pulled the club guys out of the positions in the strip club, hired Sami sometime last year, and let her hire her workers. Speed, don't let her size fool you, she cleaned out the dancers." Crusher grinned, and I couldn't imagine why, the club always handled their business.

"What are you grinning about? I can't believe they let her take over and let her clean it of its problems. That could have turned out bad—for everyone involved." Worried I may have stayed away too long.

"Asked the same shit when I got back right after she started working here. Prez liked to have taken my head off questioning him. Told me I could do what I wanted and questioned who the fuck I wanted after the spot was mine. But until then, I was to listen, not fucking be heard. After the ass chewing, we sat down and cracked open a couple of beers, then he told me he and the others did what they thought best, and it was placing Sami in total control of the strip club. Well, of course, with the backing of the MC." Crusher took a swig of his beer and continued.

"What I know ain't much, Sami and deputy pain in my ass moved here together. Sami worked at the diner and took classes over in Morrisville at the community college there. Got her degree in business, and Stroker hired her to manage Soft Tail. Heard she started working, and within a week, every stripper walked. Rock had been working, and he'd swung by the clubhouse to let them know after his shift. She walked in that day carrying those urine cups from the clinic, sat them down on the table, and told the girls they were being piss tested, and it was mandatory, and to be fair, she told them to take the test or take a walk. Their choice. Syn, Babs, and Candie were the only three to stay. The woman had replacements the next day, fresh and young college students who needed cash for school. Then she told Stroker she wanted to hire her own guys to bounce, bartend, everything to do with Soft Tail." Crusher chuckled.

"Well, at least Prez didn't let her do that? Tank was at the door when we came in, and Stem is behind the bar." Black Hawk still held a presence in the club.

"She doesn't know they're club," Jag laughed.

"What?" No way the girl was that dense.

Flirt turned from watching the stage, "Only time they can't wear their cuts, had to apply like normal folks and when they are here, no cuts." I chuckled because it was surreal that she didn't have a clue.

"No way does she not know her ass got played, seriously?" The brothers have been known to hand off bullshit.

Coast leaned back in his chair, "She doesn't hang around the club, the only time she's been there was the night you fucked her."

"Asshole, how much beer you drank, I just got back. I haven't had time to fuck anybody. I don't know the woman. Haven't been here in almost five years." Even as I said it, I turned to look around for her, I needed a better look.

"Umm…the day we buried your dad, man," Crusher whispered, I felt all their eyes on me.

"Kinda had a reason that day to let things go by without notice." Devil nudged me.

The table went quiet after Devil's words; I was sure it was because Cutter's death had entered our minds. Since my dad was never that far from my thoughts, my quietness was more to the fact of racking my memory for any reminder of the night with the little auburn-haired woman. That time between the notification of Cutter's death, then coming back to bury him was foggy on a good day. I'd just gone through the motions, so I supposed it wasn't that big of a reach not to remember her, but for some reason, being unable to remember bugged me like I should recall everything about her.

However, I'd fucked so many women from the time I'd been fifteen on that faces blended together. I couldn't even recall the nurse's face who I'd nailed in the hospital after I got back to the States and had to have therapy for my leg. But I at least remembered doing her or her doing me since she did all the work. The thought had me shifting in my chair and reaching to rearrange my package, which of course, my brothers didn't miss.

"Brother, you need to share what has that shit-eating grin on your face and you grabbing your dick." When I focused back in, all eyes were on me. Hell, if I had to shift in my seat, I damn well was going to make them shift in theirs, assholes.

"Just thinking about one of my therapy sessions for my leg." I chuckled at the looks I received.

"Goddamn, we didn't even ask how your leg is? But I know that's not what put the smirk on your face either." Coast's lifted brow was a 'share motherfucker look.'

"Leg's fine, limp a little if I get tired or been on it too long, but it doesn't slow me down any." I picked my beer up and took a pull.

"Okay, great news. Now, share the other because I know that look and when it's put together with crotch arranging, means it involves pussy, so spill, asshole."

We all laughed at Flirt's get-down-to-it attitude. "Just finished the workout on my leg and the exercises for my shoulder, showered off, placed the towel around my hips, and entered the room where they give the deep tissue massages. The female nurse who was over that area came in the first time for her to work on me and not one of the others who worked under her. She went right to my thigh, pushing deep, working out the cramps that always follow the straining exercises the leg was already put through. I relaxed while her fingers pushed deep into my thigh, but then she moved from my thigh to my dick and cupped my balls. I didn't move. I just watched her so with her eyes on me, she stopped touching my dick and started unbuttoning the top part of her nurse's getup, then the front snap of the bra released, and big titties came busting out, she grabbed them, squeezed them hard and then pulled at her nipples." I had my brothers' full attention now.

"She lifted my towel, leaned over the table, placed my cock right in the middle of those babies, and pushed them tight, wrapping my dick right up with them. Neither of us said a word, I started fucking those titties, but before I could blow my load, she pulled back and pulled a damn condom out of the pocket of her dress, which I should have known then it wasn't her first time doing this, but not like I gave a shit.

"Bitch climbed the table, straddled me, and slammed down on my dick so hard I thought the table was going to break. Rode my ass to completion, patted my chest after she climbed off me and said, "thanks, soldier," then walked out. Best damn therapy session ever."

"Sounds like she was just giving recovering soldiers a little moral support," Jag chuckled.

"Yeah, until two weeks later when one of the guy's ex-girlfriend came to pick him up and walked into the room he was in and caught Nurse Do-You-Good riding him cowgirl style."

"Ah, come on, did she lose her job over an ex-girlfriend? That's fucked up."

"Jag, she wasn't his ex until after the eight-second ride."

The brothers and I laughed, drank more, and caught up on what we'd done while apart. Nothing matched the bond we shared, and I'd missed it.

Chapter Seven

Sami

"Damn, girl, you look a little rough around the edges." I stepped back as Carly walked through the door. It was seven in the morning on a Sunday, my off day. Her insistent knocking was what pulled me out of bed.

"I closed last night like I've closed every Saturday since I took over the management at Soft Tails. Why are you here this early anyway? Didn't you say the other day that you were going to be off today too? Did I dream that shit or what?" I was bitchy because I hadn't crawled into bed until three a.m. The club closed at two a.m., and by the time I got home, watched to make sure Sue got into her place next door, locked the house up, and checked on Ally again, I'd fallen on my bed like a rock. It'd also been a restless sleep due to one man invading my dreams.

"I am off, thought I'd stop by, have coffee and breakfast with you and Spider, then maybe we could take her to the park or the movies. I even stopped and picked up donuts from Claire's Bakery." Carly sat the box down that I hadn't even noticed she had carried in.

"Was Bailey working this morning at the bakery?" I fixed the coffee pot and turned it on.

"Uh huh. She looked tired, Sami. I wish there were more we could do for her." Bailey Tolson had dropped out of college to come home when her mom, Claire, had been diagnosed with lung cancer.

"Only thing we can do is be her friend and listen. Help when we can. Bailey will get through it, she's strong." I'd been seven years old when my mother died from breast cancer, it was a loss I wouldn't wish on anyone. My dad was devastated, but he never failed to show me love, even in his pain. We'd become closer through it all; even with the demand of the club, he never wavered in spending time with me. As I grew older and ventured more on my own or with friends, we'd schedule time to spend together: movie night or even just the simplest thing as taking a walk through the woods behind the club. He helped me with homework and my hair when I was still too young to do it myself, even the boy talk, though I have to admit it was more of a 'boys are evil, they only want one thing, and I have no problem killing one if he hurts you' type discussion. Which could be the reason when I announced being pregnant, I wouldn't tell him who the father was.

"Yeah, I remember when your mom died, we were

young, you and I. And your brother, Reed, was a teenager then. Do you remember when we'd sit on each side of her on the bed and read to her? My own mother stayed so stoned that most days, she'd forget I was even there. I'd sometimes pretend that we were real sisters and your mom was mine too." I walked to the table, sat the coffee mugs down, and hugged my best friend.

"Yes, and how she'd laugh when we'd make up words to replace the ones we didn't know." We both chuckled.

"Reading romance books at seven."

"Mom would stop us, take the book, and tell us she was tired and needed to nap. You know it was because we were going to hit a racy piece in the book," I shook my head, "I think I was like fourteen when I thought about that one day when I came across one of those books in the back of a closet and took it to my room to read. Between what we witnessed on occasion in the club and the books, it was like having a visual sex ed class." As we reminisced about my mom, Carly opened the box of donuts, and we dug in. Laughing at some of the good times we had, frowning at some of the bad. But at the end of the day, the club was family, no matter what went on. And there was plenty.

"Not like we would have known then what most of the words meant. We were still young enough that the men and women sheltered us from it. The day your dad caught us reading when he'd come to check on your mom, and she was asleep, but we were still reading the book out loud. I thought he was mad at us because his face was puckered up, and he was biting his lip when he took the book from us, but no, you'd just read "his hand held her breast" before he'd walked in. Then you asked him if the man was holding the lady's boobies so she could put on her bra." Carly lifted her cup to her mouth and smiled before taking a drink.

"Uh huh, and then he burst out laughing when you said it was nice for men to do that," I laughed, remembering.

"Yeah, but he stopped laughing when I said I was going to have a boyfriend that likes to do that too." I watched Carly's smile turn into a frown as she looked down at the table. She smiled when she raised her head back up to look at me, but it looked as if she had to fight to keep the smile.

"What?"

"Just thinking how Wallace liked to help a lot of women put their bras on. And my mom slept with anyone who'd give her a toke. What a pair, exactly alike, no wonder they couldn't get along for more than five minutes. You know, his hands probably touched more breasts than a worker's at one of Tyson's chicken plants."

"That was a bad affinity," I brought my hands to my face and muffled the laughter. Carly's dad had always been a piece of work.

"Please. It's the truth, the man was a dog, and he should be put out of his misery." I stopped laughing and looked at her.

"Are you ever going to tell me why you hate the man so much?" Her eyes met mine, and she shook her head.

"He's not worth the breath. I hope wherever he is, it's hot, it will prepare him for when he dies and spends eternity in hell." Carly pushed her chair back and stepped to the coffee pot for a refill. Her way of letting me know that she was done with the subject. We'd been friends a long time; she'd tell me when she was ready. We each held secrets—hers about Stone—mine about Ally's dad. It'd been three days since I saw him. I knew I wouldn't be lucky enough for that to last, our town wasn't tiny, but it wasn't the big city either. Eventually, my luck would run out. I just needed to figure out if/or how I was going to tell him. And wondered if he'd care he had a daughter. Then, my dad, that was going to be fun. Which reminded me.

"Hey, Dad's coming the week after next for his usual visit."

"Wild Bill coming by himself this time, or is one of the others riding with him? He shouldn't be riding by himself, Sami."

"Reed's riding in with him this time." Carly sneered at this information. "Stop it. Get over it, it's been a few years."

"Does there have to be something wrong? His breathing pisses me off. He picked on us day and night growing up. He, too, could be used against your dad. But oh no, he is a man. He's an Enforcer for your dad. Boo hoo hoo, I mean really, when does he find the time to stop looking at himself in the mirror long enough to take care of a club?" I was too late to stop Carly when the footsteps coming down the hall registered. "Self-centered asshole is what he is."

"That's a bad word, Aunt Carly." My daughter entered the kitchen, rubbing her eyes as she took a chair at the table.

"Yeah, yeah, shortstop." Ally giggled while Carly sat back down.

"Want to go to the park with Aunt Carly today?" I knew that question would wake my daughter up, she loved the park.

"Yay! Can we go now?" Ally lowered her hands, all but vibrating in her seat, and looked at Carly.

"First, some breakfast." I opened the cabinet and pulled out the pancake mix and syrup. "Then clothes." I may have rolled out of bed tired, but as I looked at my daughter and her excitement, tired had no place to exist when I had the time to spend with her.

"Well, look. Church must be in service at Soft Tails." I looked out the passenger side window and realized immediately what Carly was talking about. The parking lot was full of bikes.

"Must have something special going on. That's the only time they use the club when it's closed." Soft tails closed down on Sundays and Mondays, it had been one of the changes I had requested from Black Hawk when I was hired. Sundays and Mondays were slow days; Sunday was spent with family for most people, and Monday, most were getting back into their workweek. They hadn't fought me on it. Actually, to think back, I'd gotten most of what I wanted. Well, except for hiring my own people to work with. Oh, I got to hire them, held interviews and everything—I just happened to hire the guys from the club who applied for the positions. The leadership thought they pulled one over, and that I didn't know. I knew, went with it, and didn't say a word. I felt the smile spread across my face as I thought back on it.

"That has you smiling? I don't know how you work for them. Arrogant pric—" I cut her off, little ears catch-all.

"Don't forget who is in the back seat. Carly, they aren't bad, I don't know why you are so against all that is MC, we were raised in one. And besides, you own a bike, for God's sake. Do you think that would have come about if you were raised in an everyday household: Mom, Dad, siblings, and a mini-van?" We'd had this conversation more than once over the years living here.

"Easy for you to say. You were the club princess, and even here, the Black Hawks treat you good. Sami, we might have been raised in Haven MC, but it wasn't a haven for me like it was for you. You're the president's daughter. I'm the daughter of a dead club whore who took up with a p.r.i.c.k.," Carly spelled, and it made me smile, "then she used her pregnancy to make her his ol' lady, neither of them took that serious considering they never stopped sleeping with others." I watched her hands tighten and clench on the steering wheel.

"Carly, so your parents weren't perfect. Still doesn't explain why you are bitter toward the MCs. Help me understand." The change in her happened shortly after we moved here, but she never would confess what took place. She'd had lousy parents, but my dad and my mom, when she was still living, treated her good just like they did me. And considering the drugs and criminal activities that I figured they were involved in when I grew old enough to understand what exactly was happening around me, it could have gone the other way. But even with that, the members and the few ol' ladies around treated us well.

"I grew up, got a clue." She was evading. Her M.O. to everything she didn't want to discuss. "And it's got nothing to do with my bike. I like the freedom it offers. They're fun to ride. I tried to get you to learn when I did." Yes, she had. And the reason I didn't was dumb, and I would never admit it out loud, but if I closed my eyes, I could still see my mother's smile for my dad when she'd get on his bike with him and hold on tight as they pulled away. The only bike I'd ever sat on was my dad's when he would take me for a ride.

"I want a bike like Aunt Carly's." See? Little ears pick up all.

"You do, huh? Maybe your mom will get one for you when you get a little older. Whatcha think, short stack?" Ally and I laughed, Carly had been calling her different short-whatever since Ally was born.

"I don't know about that, Ally. Don't listen to Aunt Carly." I wasn't sure my daughter needed to be on a motorcycle, she was a big enough daredevil.

"That's 'k, my daddy will buy me a bike." I whipped my head around to look at her. Days had passed, and nothing after the initial daddy announcement she made. I'd so hoped she had forgotten and moved on. No such luck. I was going to let it pass so she would start on the whole business once again, but Carly was no help.

"Shorty poo, how will a daddy buy you a bike? Girls

don't need a guy to get her one, she can buy one herself." My mouth opened to speak, but Ally's next words had me shutting it.

"My daddy is going to ride a bike just like my papa does?"

I turned back as if to look out the side window again, but it was more so Carly or my daughter didn't see the tears that rose in my eyes. Her words made me realize I couldn't keep them apart, no matter what the outcome. One thing I knew for sure, he could forget me all he wanted, but if he hurt my daughter, he'd never forget me again—he'd remember every time he went to pee and his balls weren't there.

"Sami?" I looked over to Carly as she glanced between me and the road. "You got quiet, what's goin' on in your head, bikes, and daddies?" The last part said low enough only I heard it.

My dad wasn't the only one I didn't tell who Ally's father was, and I wasn't ready to tell him now. "Sure, I'll tell you everything as soon as you tell me why your attitude changed on MCs." I opened the door as soon as she stopped the car in the driveway of my house.

When I opened the back door to help Ally out, Carly was out and looked over the top of the car, "My issue."

"Yes, just like me, you hold secrets." I walked toward the door, Carly and Ally following. "You staying for lunch?"

"Yeah, if you make pizza."

"God, you act five." I shook my head and walked into the house.

"That's why shortcake and I are besties."

And just like that, everything was back to normal. At least for a little while.

Chapter Eight

Speed

"Sorry, it took me a few days to work my way here. You should have been the first stop I made when I reached town." I looked down, wasn't expecting an answer, and moved closer until I stood directly in front of the headstone. I ran my hand over the cold granite and took a deep breath, inhaling the morning air.

"Things have changed since I been gone. The club's changing. I'm sure you've chuckled a few times over it going legit. Never thought I'd see the day, at least not until me and the others took over.

"Got Church in a bit, guess I'll get caught up on it all. They're holding it at Soft Tails because the whole club is attending today. After Church, we'll be celebrating my coming home for good. You probably know they did it for the others when they got back too, but I expect this one will be a little wilder since we're all home now. Won't be the same, though, without you standing to the side watching and listening to everything going on around you.

"Fuck, if the guys heard me talking with you… I just can't seem to let you go yet. I know you are saying it's been long enough, but you being out by yourself, no one knowing why—that's what keeps me from letting you rest. Letting myself rest.

"I'll figure it out, you taught me well. Probably should be going so I'm not late, and the Prez kicks my ass. Miss you, Dad. Hope you're getting to ride often and the road's paved and open." My fist hit the granite, and I turned and walked back to my bike.

When I pulled into the lot at Soft Tails, the only bikes in the lot were the dads' and the guys'. I backed my bike up at the end of the line, dismounted, and headed in.

"How's it going, Speed? Went by your house to see if you wanted to ride in with us and you were gone," Crusher yelled when I walked in.

"Went to the cemetery." He nodded and walked to the table where Stroker was sitting with Preacher, Romeo, Flyboy, and Cruz. The table was set so the officers could face the rest of the members while they sat in chairs facing the main table. That's where Devil, Flirt, Coast, and Jag sat. Crusher and I joined on the front row.

"Wanted to talk to you before the rest of the members got here, Speed and the rest of you too. First, the club will slowly turn over to you when we feel each of you is ready to take the position you will hold. Before you go gettin' your backs up, it's because we are one hundred percent legit." Even though the guys had pretty much filled me in, hearing it from the leadership was kind of a shock. The only response from us was nods.

"We will go over the specifics when Church officially starts. Now, Speed, your spot is vacant. We held it that way after Cutter died so when you came back, it would be waiting. We talked when you showed up this week, and you will be the first to take over your position." The others stood and started slapping me on the back.

"Sit down, boys. I wasn't done. Speed, we know our friend and brother taught you well. You'll be an asset to us as an Enforcer. We may be legal now, but we have to keep our presence known and show no weakness, just as before. We'll support our brothers from other clubs we have good relations with. We may follow the laws as business goes, but that doesn't mean we'll let another club move into our territory, nor will we show any weakness in taking care of the club if that were to occur.

"That being said, we're going to give you time to acclimate back into the club. You will work as Enforcer on an interim basis. Once we feel you are ready, the position is totally yours, and you will represent this club in the full capacity of the position."

"So I need to prove worthy of the position, is that what you are saying, Prez?" I felt like I was being put through a test.

"Yes, but it is nothing the others won't be put through. They will just have more time to learn. Your spot is open, waiting for you to fill it." I nodded, to a point I understood them not wanting to throw me into the spot, but in another, it felt as if they knew something and were waiting for me to figure it out. My gut had never failed me, and I was sure it wasn't failing me now.

Cruz, Coast's dad, stood and walked toward me. "We'll walk through things when you're ready. Ask questions, whatever you need from me, Speed, I'm here." I stood, and we did the man hug thing just as the door opened and a few members walked in.

"Brothers, Church in fifteen." Stroker and the rest stood and started talking to a few of the men who came in. It didn't take long for the place to fill and for the meeting to get underway.

I sat and listened to get caught up on everything I'd missed out on since the last time I was home. After Stroker had called order to the meeting, the officers did a run-through on all businesses the Black Hawks owned. Profits, which showed the club's earnings were strong and gains salient. How the club had increased its membership over the last few years was more balanced with numbers between older and younger members.

Soft Tails had shown a nice increase in business with the chick as a manager; profits were up, which meant losses were down. A big part of that was evidently due to the decrease in fighting in the strip club, with no extra cost replacing broken tables and chairs.

For a moment, the mention of the petite little woman crossed my mind. I'd caught myself the last couple of days thinking about the brief encounter with her and Coast's words of me fucking her. As she walked away, her tight ass in the black jeans was a pic that entered my mind several times. Even fully clothed, she was the whole package, I could imagine unwrapping that package and finding soft skin under the touch of my fingers and lips. The way she'd withered and squirmed as I teased her with my mouth. Pulling back just as I felt the start of her body quaking toward orgasm, then bringing her back up to the breaking point and starting it all over again until my need for release pressed hard against me. Then I'd take her hard, driving my cock deep until there was no space between us. Until my name came from her lips like a prayer. And fuck, for all I remember about her, I could have already done it all.

Christ, I shook my head and glanced around. Yeah, that thought needed to get the fuck out of my mind because sitting in a room with forty-plus bikers and no woman in attendance to play off the fact you were sporting a hard-on that could bust concrete if you let it out of its confines, was in no way a good thing. I needed to sink mindlessly into a pussy. Not for lack of some of the hang-arounds from Saturday's party.

I'd only been back for a few days, and the only relief I'd had that wasn't hand related was a blowjob. Crusher had been right about Lindy being a horny little thing, though. That night the six of us had been in the room right off from the main room where the party was going strong. The club called it the game room since that was where the pool table and a few tables used to play cards sat. We'd had a pool game going when Lindy had sashayed in to watch. Well, it had started out as her watching—until playing pool was forgotten, and the table was used for a different game. Devil closed the door to the room, and Flirt grabbed Lindy by the hips, turned her, and bent her over the table. Her short skirt was pushed up, and he slapped her ass. It hadn't taken long for the chick to start moaning every time his palm touch the cheek of her ass.

"You want us, bitch?" This was a new side of Flirt I hadn't witnessed before, and when she didn't answer him fast enough, he kneed her legs apart until she was spread as wide as they would allow, then the next swat he administered was right on her pussy.

"Yes!" she yelled, but it wasn't in pain as we all witnessed the shiver work through her body and her pussy glisten from her orgasm.

Fuck it, I hadn't had any type of sex in a few weeks, so I'm not proud to admit that we had every intention of taking part in what she offered.

"All of us, Lindy? You got to say so, or we stop," Flirt said and looked at each of us.

"Yes, all six of you, Sir." Damn, not like we hadn't done it before. We'd shared everything growing up, it may have started with our toys before it turned into women, but we'd shared those too. I knew that at least two cheerleaders from our high school had taken the six of us on. It was when I first understood the saying "rode hard and hung up wet."

Pants were unzipped, dicks were out, and Lindy was naked, straddling Devil on the table already fitted with a condom and Flirt knelt behind her before it registered that we were really going to get down to it. Crusher, Coast, Jag, and I moved two to each side of the table.

"Put these on her nipples, she likes that bite of pain, doncha, Lindy?" Flirt had pulled silver clamps with a chain connecting them from his pocket.

"Seriously, you carry those around?" Talk about prepared.

Flirt turned his head toward me and winked, "You know, as the military taught us—always be prepared."

Devil had worked fast, attaching the clamps that reminded me of a tiny set of trigger clamps I had in the garage with the tightening mechanism on them. Lindy wiggled as Devil fitted them snugly to her nipples, and Flirt smacked her ass and told her to stop moving as he suited up his dick and began coating it with lube, then worked the lube on Lindy to loosen up her tight back hole.

"Take Devil's cock in your pussy, now!" Flirt commanded, and Lindy slammed down on Devil, engulfing him in one motion. Then Flirt pushed her forward and pushed into her ass, filling her.

She was definitely enjoying herself as she moaned and yelled, "Move, please!"

Devil held the chain to the clamp in his hand while helping to hold Lindy so she didn't fall over when she motioned us other four closer to the table, and the fun began as she took turns pumping our cocks and sucking on them.

Each time it was my turn, she took my dick a little more into her mouth until the head hit the back of her throat.

Flirt pounded into her ass, moving her with him, so she rode Devil at the same time. The girl had skills and was flexible as hell, too, leaning over to reach each of us standing on the sides of the table.

My last go around had me shooting down her throat, and as she worked back to the others finishing each off, Flirt pushed her down on Devil and slammed into her ass at the same time Devil released the clamps on her nipples. Her yell of pleasure bounced off the walls. I knew there was no way no one in the main room missed it, even with the music blasting.

The door opened, and Tank stood there with a smirk on his face, "Fuckers, we play pool on that goddamn table, so make sure you clean it up." Then he closed the door.

The club had done away with the club whores that were always around, the only one left who stayed at the club was Daisy. She'd been a constant in the club as I grew up, but the guys informed me her role now, other than for some of the older single members' pleasure, she took care of the place and cooked for the officers when they were at the clubhouse doing business. She was also in charge of the hang-arounds when there was a party, making sure one, the women attending were legal, and two, no drama got started between them. The men there had no use for a pussy if it came with teeth, ready to clamp down on your dick like a chew toy and not allowing anyone else to play with it.

"That was the last order of business. The floor is open

if anyone has questions or wants to bring up new business for discussion. Everyone knows we are holding the meeting here in Soft Tails because of Speed's return, and we need the room for the party. The ol' ladies will be here in about fifteen minutes to join us, and they are bringing food."

When I heard my name, I shook my head, realizing I missed some of what was covered in the meeting. Great, I hope this wasn't part of my fucking test to see if I was fit to take the Enforcer position. But at least I had fifteen minutes to get rid of my now raging hard-on, which all started because of thinking of the tight ass in black jeans. It may have been wrong but fuck it, someone needed to be blamed for causing me to zone out on a meeting.

I looked over at Crusher when I felt his elbow on my side. "Take a nice trip there, Speed?" I wanted to smack that damn grin right off his face. Should've known one of the fuckers would have caught me.

"Asshole," was the only word said as I stood and headed toward the restroom. It was going to be one long ass day.

Chapter Nine

Sami

Sleep failed to come to me as I lay in bed, the thoughts of a man I really didn't know haunted me. I needed to tell him about his daughter, but how? It wasn't something I could just go up to him and say, "I know you don't remember me, fucking me, but would you like to meet your daughter?" Yeah, that would go over well.

Pounding the pillow and flopping from side to side hadn't helped either. I'd do the right thing and tell him. Three weeks after my one and only night at the Black Hawks' clubhouse, I'd woken that morning sick, my stomach turning over, sending me right into the bathroom to hug the porcelain god. When it continued each morning for three days in a row, I told myself it was the flu. Another week later, I steeled myself and headed to the clinic, denial still my closest friend. While I waited for the doctor to come in to talk to me after I'd given blood, peed in a cup, and been examined, I still held on to the denial.

But when the doctor came in, flipped the chart, and verified the pee test positive for pregnancy, denial left, replaced with Mr. Mistake because I'd been on the pill and the baby's daddy had worn a condom. I'd left out the part that he'd worn a condom at least half a dozen times in the one night because his words were, "Sleep was overrated."

"Ms. Borelli, though there is near zero percent chance when both protections are used, they aren't one hundred percent, nothing is. I estimate from the time of your last period, you are around four weeks. Do you have a gynecologist here, or do you need me to recommend one?"

I'd shook my head while she continued to advise me about the risks of taking the pill while pregnant but that my OB/Gyn would take care of that part.

It had all been scary and frightening to an almost nineteen-year-old girl, but the first time I felt the baby move, nothing in life had prepared me for the emotions that surfaced, and somehow I knew it would all work out. I would do anything to make sure it did. And I had.

I'd even gone back to the Black Hawks' clubhouse to tell the man I'd only known as Speed that he was going to be a father, and I was under no assumption he would jump for joy. I was only giving him a choice if he wanted to be in the child's life—I'd owed him that much. But when I was told he was gone, I'd left with no explanation as to why I was asking for him even though they'd asked for a reason. So he'd just have to accept the fact he had a daughter. It was really all I wanted him to do, accept her, I didn't need to be a part of the equation. But as sleep started to grab hold, I fell completely under on the thought, *I wanted to matter to him too.* Crazy after one night with a man I didn't really know.

My eyes opened when the body I was draped across began to shake. I looked up through my lashes, and the man's face in the shadowed light of the moon held a grimace. The shout of, "Get to cover" broke the silence in the room and had me frozen in place, then the arm wrapped around me tightened, leaving me no other choice but to wake him or stay still and see if his dream would pass and he would go back to sleeping soundly.

He mumbled unclear words until he yelled, "Noooo!" The way it was said sent chills over me, and I realized whatever he dreamt was not easing nor fading back into his brain's recesses. So I moved my arm from my side slowly, placed my hand lightly on his chest, and began to rub. His breath exhaled, and his breathing began to settle, his body relaxing more with every motion of my hand. My touch soothing him.

I don't know how long I watched this man sleep, but I'd continued to run my hand over his chest and arms, then back again. I caught myself tracing his tattoos as if outlining them. I hadn't seen his back, but assumed it too must have held a tattoo since almost every space from his neck down was nothing but tattoo after tattoo. They were beautiful and colorful, and each probably held a meaning as to why he had it done. Too nice to be just ones chosen to fill an empty spot.

When his arm went lax and dropped away, releasing its hold on me, I bolted. In my head, I explained it as I had to get home, that was all. But looking back—I bolted from sure fear. The fear that if I stayed and woke up beside this man, there'd be no turning back. I hadn't just soothed him—his touch on my skin from the time we'd entered the room had not only excited me—it had burned through me, leaving me with the knowledge he had the power to crush me.

"Mama? Why are you crying?" The hand shaking me startled me awake.

"Oh, honey, I wasn't crying. I must have something in my eyes that is making them water." I wiped my cheeks with my hands, sat up in bed, and hoped my daughter would accept the lame excuse. That's when I noticed Carly leaning on the doorframe, eyebrow cocked, looking at me.

I focused on my daughter's scrunched-up face as she examined me. "You need coffee, Aunt Carly made it. She made me breakfast too." Ally leaned in and lowered her voice, which for her wasn't nearly low enough to keep Carly from hearing, "It was yucky, the scrambled eggs moved on my plate. They don't move when you fix 'em." Carly covered the grin on her face as she sipped from her cup.

"Sorry, honey. You want me to cook you something else?" I smiled as Ally looked at me, then at Carly, and back at me.

"Can I have a pop-tart?"

"Sure, baby." She hugged me and started for the door. We both watched her leave and didn't speak until we heard her feet running down the hall.

"Wanna tell me what that was about before?" My daughter may have let my tears go, but I should have known my friend would not.

"Nope, wanna tell me the deal between you and Crusher?" I rose from the bed and headed toward the bathroom door.

"Nope." Carly straightened from the doorframe.

"Well, there you go. Are you on shift today?"

"Yep, going home to shower and put my uniform on. Thanks for dinner, the movie, and the couch."

"Anytime." I stopped before entering the bathroom and turned back to face her. Years of being friends taught me one thing, I knew when she had more to say and was trying to figure out how to say it. "What? I know that look."

"Going to tell him? Tell her?"

"Carly, who are you talking about? Him, her?" My stomach flipped when the look of 'giving me a fuckin' break' crossed her face.

"I saw him, he's the one, isn't he?"

"When, where, and how?" I was stalling, she knew, I knew it.

"Told you I was out at the clubhouse with the sheriff, talking with Mr. Davis. Evidently, he'd just got back. Saw him before we left. Did you honestly think when that man looked at me, fuck, Sami, I don't think identical twins could look that much alike?"

"Going to take a shower. Errands to run today: grocery store, post office. The fun stuff. Be safe today." I walked into the bathroom and shut the door, effectively stopping the conversation. Well, on my part. My friend had more to say.

"Might want to tell him. Soon too. Though I think

they are a few cells short in the brain department, pretty sure he's going to see the resemblance. Truthfully, I don't know how any of the Black Hawk MC, who have seen, her haven't picked up on it. That is one thing about club life that stuck with me—family is family—they don't let theirs go far."

It went quiet, and I reached and turned the knobs to start my shower. Carly was right, more than she even knew. And me… Well…

Out of time came to mind as I stepped into the shower.

Chapter Ten

Speed

My watch read noon, and I ran my hand over my head, then rubbed my thigh as I raised from the squatted position. I'd woken at three a.m., sleep a distant memory as it was most nights. From then till now, I'd gotten a lot of things done. The room with my dad's boxed things was the first place I'd hit after coffee had been made.

The room now was sorted into two parts: one, things that needed to be given away, the other, mementos of Cutter I would keep. I'd lived with the man my whole life, but going through his things, left me wondering if I'd actually known him. We were as close as father and son could be. Yet I'd felt his loss every time I pulled a picture I had drawn, a test paper with an A+ circled on the top, he and me in a photo from my graduation—his arm over my shoulder and a smile spread across his face. He'd even had pictures that reflected the stages of my childhood as I aged, the last photo in that group was the day I left for the Marines. One of the other men must have taken the picture because Cutter stood off to the side in the picture with the focus being me with the others: Crusher, Flirt, Jag, Coast, and Devil. I'd been the first to head away from the club and the last to come back to it. What caught me off guard in the photo had been the expression and posture of my dad—they'd showed the proudness that he couldn't speak aloud of.

He'd been a tough father, keeping emotions in check, and he raised me the same. Not without love or that he'd never shown me he cared—it was just never said aloud but always there.

After that chore was finished, I found nothing in his things that pointed to why he would have been out on his own at night one day. Not like I thought anything would be there. I'd just hoped to answer a few questions that bothered me about it all.

I placed the tools back in their spot at the workstation. After the bedroom cleaning, I came out to the garage and removed some of the damaged parts to his bike, so I could put a list together of the parts I was going to need or rebuild to put it back in riding shape.

"Hey, Speed, what you up to?" Crusher and Jag walked into the garage.

"Wow, man, you've been busy." Jag bent and looked at the parts laid out on the tarp.

"Seeing what I'm looking at with getting it back in

running condition," I shrugged, opened the Gojo container, and began cleaning the grease off my hands.

"Kinda what we stopped by to talk about." Crusher sat on the stool off to the side.

"Shoot, what's on your mind." My curiosity peaked at his words.

"How you'd feel about opening a shop?" Jag stood and turned toward us.

"Club has a garage. Why would we want to open another?"

"Speed, not a garage, a shop. One to make custom bikes."

"Are you talking the six of us, Crusher? And do you think we could make a go of it? Enough demand, considering we would only be able to build four to six a year, depending on what the clientele asked for." We grew up working on bikes, our fathers and the other men in the club taught us everything we knew about bikes.

"Yeah, we already have four guys who live in Cali and ride leisurely that want a custom job to show off. And more money than they have sense. We figured with the six of us working it, your estimate on how many we could do in a year is close. So?" Crusher grinned.

"You fuckers had this all worked out. When did you plan on telling me?"

"Now." Jag laughed.

"Asshole." My eyebrows cocked, waiting for them to explain.

"The building behind Hawk's came open, the club was

going to buy it and extend the garage out, but Dad said we could have it for our business if we wanted." Crusher shrugged.

"Hmmm—" I looked around my garage, it was a spacious three-bay. It held every tool imaginable and was a helluva lot closer than driving to town to go to work. "What about here?"

"Here?" Jag looked around. "Might have to build on, at least for storage of parts and shit."

"I agree," Crusher stood and began walking around the garage.

"Other than building an addition like Jag said, no cost for the building, no tools to buy, and other than purchasing parts, we could pretty much start the business tomorrow." I smiled, it would be the closest to working with Cutter on bikes as I could get. Working with my friends in the same garage where I had some of the best memories of time spent with my dad.

"Let's do it," Flirt said as he stepped in with Coast and Devil behind him.

"It works for our needs." Coast looked around.

"We'd only waited for you to get back to complete the deal." Devil walked up and slapped my back.

"Well, now, the only thing we need is a name, and I will file my first official paperwork as the attorney for the club when I file for our business license along with trademarking the name." Jag smiled at us.

"Sons of Black Hawk Custom Rides." It hit me as I looked at each one of my friends and took the smacks to my back as a unanimous yes.

Looked like Black Hawk MC was going to have a new business.

The lot at B&B was full as I parked the cage toward the end of an aisle. The ol' ladies' food had run out, and it was time to stock my place. I'd had a productive day between clearing the room, breaking down the bike, and making plans for a business with my best friends. All in all, not a bad day.

After the guys had left, I showered, dressed, and headed to town. I swung by the diner and ate a burger and fries before I made my way to the store. No way was I going to this place hungry. Years ago, I'd learned that lesson when I'd had my first place and had thrown out more of what I bought than I had eaten.

Hadn't taken long to fill the cart, I only had one more aisle to backtrack to, the cereal, my weakness too. I ate plenty of meat and vegetables to keep my physique prime. However, I'd never been able to make myself eat healthy cereals, I enjoyed the shit I'd eaten as a kid: Fruit Loops, Lucky Charms, and my favorite, Captain Crunch.

When I headed down the aisle, I noticed the little body hanging onto the top shelf with one hand and reaching the other to get a box from the shelf. The kid was stretched on her tippy toes, and my only thought was that was so not going to end well.

"Darlin', you need some help with that?" I wanted to grab her but didn't think a grown man grabbing a little girl and scaring the shit out of her would be such a good idea, but it happened anyway when I spoke because her foot slipped, and she was headed down the shelves.

I grabbed her around the waist and set her down quickly, then reached and snagged the box she was trying to grab off the shelf. I turned and looked down at her.

"This what you wanted?" I hadn't paid close attention to her until she looked up at me.

"Yep, thanks, mister." She reached her small hand out for the box, but I didn't move, I just stared at her. The little girl with my face, hair, and eyes. Fuck me. No doubt entered my mind about her parentage. I imagined I'd have looked just like her at that age if I'd been a girl. Considering how she was dressed in jeans, a t-shirt, and boots on her feet, her hair and facial features were the only things to give away that she was a girl. A beautiful little girl who no doubt belonged to me.

"Can I have my cereal? I said thanks like my momma told me to when people help." Her eyes stared into mine, and I watched her eyebrows draw together in thought, and she sucked her lip between her teeth.

"Sure, darlin'. Where's your mommy or daddy at?" It was wrong, but I wanted to know what the little girl had been told.

"Momma forgot to get my favorite, so she sent me while she was going to get her female things. Whatever that means?" Damn, if she wasn't a cutie and she hadn't been done talking either.

"I don't gots a daddy. He's gone. You got a daddy?"

"No, my daddy is gone too." I continued to watch her

face as she watched me. Then, after she looked up and down the aisle, she leaned closer to me and lowered her voice.

"Benji said I couldn't go to the party at school for dads because I don't have one. Did you miss daddy parties too?" I had no clue who Benji was, but the kid needed his ass kicked. I may not have known this little creature existed until this moment, but no one, and I mean no one, would ever hurt her, she was fucking mine.

"That right, huh? Whatcha your momma say to that?" It was wrong to pump the kid when I should have let her go to her mother before her mother came looking for her. We'd have a conversation about what was mine, but it wouldn't be in a damn grocery store.

Her voice lowered, "I punched him in the nose, and momma said I wasn't to hit people even if they said ugly things?"

"You did good. Nice job, slugger." Yeah didn't care about the father of the fuckin' year, my girl would take no shit from anyone.

"I'm spider, not slugger."

"Spider?" Christ, I had no clue about little girls.

"Spider monkey."

"Oh, because you climb?" I chuckled when she just stared at me.

"Not just that. I got black hair, and I am fast. Perry said it's because I'm evil like them."

"Did he now?" By my calculations, the ass-kicking numbers were going to skyrocket. Fuckers hadn't said a goddamn word.

"Yep. You got kids?" The same color eyes looked back at me. How to answer this one?

"Sure do."

"A boy or girl? Benji said my daddy probably left because I was a girl."

"Benji says a lot of shit, doesn't he?" Yeah, hope Benji's dad had fucking life insurance, Benji's mom could be a rich woman.

"That's a bad word. Aunt Carly says bad words too. She called Benji a little bastard, and momma yelled at her. But don't tell my momma, she don't know I heard her, and it's a bad word too." I bit down on the inside of my jaw to hold back the laugh only because of the serious look on my daughter's face. My daughter, fucking unreal.

"Sure thing, darlin', you better go find your momma before she hunts for you." Her mother and I would have a chat after I took care of a few other things first.

"'K," she said and took off down the aisle. I watched until she turned out of view, then grabbed a box of the cereal and chuckled—Captain Crunch—yeah, she was mine.

After I had checked out and loaded the bags into the back of the truck, I got in the cab and waited. I wanted to see the woman, my daughter's mother. Sami walked off at the club when she recognized me. I might not have recognized her then, but it came back to me. And wasn't that convenient since it was her who had me up at three in the morning.

I remembered everything: the feel of her skin, the way her mouth tasted when I kissed her, the taste of her juices as I licked and sucked at her, bringing her to orgasm. But even with all that, what I remember most was *her* touch. Her fingers tracing my tattoos, the way she ran her hand over me, pushing the dreams back that haunted me. The faces of my comrades as they died, the enemy I killed in retaliation, it was at night when it would sneak in to torment me. She made it go away, giving me peace for the first time since I'd gone to the desert.

Motion at the front doors had me sitting up straighter in the seat. There she was, the auburn-haired woman with the little girl with black flowing hair. I watched them push the wheeled cart to their car, fill the trunk with bags, and then get in and drive off. My truck not far behind them. I followed at a distance until they pulled into a driveway to a small house, then I drove past. I now knew where they lived and would be back. But first, back home, and then over to the clubhouse to get some answers. It'd been kept for almost five years, a few more hours wasn't going to matter.

I'd laughed out loud on my way back when it hit me that, like the encounter with her mother, other than Spider, I didn't get her name either.

Chapter Eleven

Speed

The door to the clubhouse hit the wall and bounced back to close on its own as I walked in. The brothers that sat in the room looked at me, but not a word was said, which told me my face must have reflected my intentions.

I'd already gone to my home and put the food away, not because I was afraid it would spoil, but more to calm my ass down some before my head exploded. Every emotion flowed through me as I'd driven back from town. Pain from the betrayal and deceit of my brothers, which quickly turned into anger toward them and against the woman who had kept my daughter from me. When I stepped out of the truck at my home, my head was ready to explode, so I took that small amount of time to do something normal before going to the club.

As I walked down the hallway toward the office, the stop by the cabin had been a waste as my fists clenched at my sides. I didn't stop to knock, I grabbed the knob and threw the door open, and walked straight into the office, catching Stroker, Flyboy, Preacher, Cruz, and Romeo off guard. Stroker sat behind his desk, and the other men sat in chairs in front of him, each with their head turned toward the door I just barreled through.

"How fucking long have you known, all of you?" No way everyone who happened to be in the clubhouse hadn't heard me yell, but I would have had to care to give a shit.

"Close the door and take a seat, Speed," Stroker said and motioned to a chair to the side of the desk. His voice was calm and normal, considering I about took his office door off its hinges.

"Answer me?" I said as I turned and shut the door.

"Sit, now. I can tell you are upset but don't forget I am the president of this club, and you will have respect for the fucking position whether you don't have respect for the man. Take. A. Fucking. Seat. Now." He leaned back and crossed his arms over his chest, and waited. The others hadn't said a word but held identical poses.

"I will stand here until someone answers me because if I get closer and don't like the answer, I could easily crack a few heads." I held up my hand when Cruz's mouth opened to speak, cutting him off, "Before you go spewing club rules and shit as the Enforcer for Black Hawk, save it. I will kick ass and take names if I don't like the fucking answers," I looked directly at Stroker, "and I say it with all respect to this club and the position you hold, I'll let you know if I have respect for the man when you're done speaking." My heart felt like it was going to come through my chest as I looked at them and waited. I didn't get the immediate answers I wanted, what I got was five men looking back with smiles spreading across their faces.

"What the fuck are you smiling about? I just said I would kick your asses if I didn't like your answers."

The door flew open, and Crusher, Flirt, Jag, Coast, and Devil brought up the rear. They came to a halt when they surveyed the standoff in the room.

"Has everyone in this club lost their fucking minds on whose office this is? I don't want an answer to that question because I'm going to answer it for you." Stroker stood, his smile was gone, and the mask he wore was the one I remembered from our youth when we'd sat in chairs in this office and had our collective asses chewed off for some shit we'd done.

Finger pointed at me, Stroker motioned toward the chair by his desk again. "You, there, now if you want your goddamn answers," then he pointed at the others and motioned toward the couches pushed against the wall. "Plant your asses there, and if one of you opens your damn mouth without one of the other officers or me speaking to you, you'll get a lesson on how we still hold this club and why other clubs don't fuck with us." He stood, waiting, as we each moved to sit. Once we'd sat, Stroker took his seat once again.

"Now, nice to see you aren't going to have an issue

questioning Crusher when he takes over as president. I worried, we all did," his arm stretched and waved to encompass the other officers, "about you boys being too close and just going with the flow instead of asking questions or holding each other responsible for the jobs you will hold in this club. That being said, let us get to what brought you barreling into this office ready to mow down each of us.

"I'm assuming you ran into your daughter today, Speed?" Without turning in their direction, I felt my friends' eyes on me. "Hear me out before anyone speaks," Stroker's hand raised palm out, halting me and probably the others too from talking. "We didn't know at first. Right before your father's accident, we were contacted by Haven MC's president. I'd known Wild Bill before he took over when his dad was killed, he'd just come back from the military, the same battalion I was attached to, and he was married when he came back. Haven had always been rivals of Black Hawk because his old man was a mean sonofabitch. The Haven club are one percenters, which you boys know. But while dealing with moving drugs, some of the members started using more of their product. When your members are drugged up, that is when the clubs become vulnerable. Wild Bill called and wanted to know if we would let two of Haven's women come into our territory while he figured out what was going on in his club. It seems his VP, along with a couple of others in the club, didn't like Wild Bill taking over for his dad, nor when the club got worse with the drug use, the fact he was going to clean that up. They planned a little coup per se, but Wild Bill caught wind. That's why he asked to put the women here. He didn't want them used as pawns while he figured out exactly who was involved. One is his daughter, the other the VP's." Stroker paused and looked around the room.

"What the fuck does this have to do with my goddamn daughter?" Then it clicked, and I raised my hand to stop Stroker. "Are you saying Sami is Wild Bill Borelli's daughter? My daughter's grandfather?" Stroker looked as if he was trying to hold back a laugh, and when I looked at the others, they, too, were biting the insides of their mouths, their eyes gleaming with humor. My friends' expressions would have been comical if I weren't shocked at my fucking luck. "Fuck me, it's all true. And you bastards want to laugh. There is not a damn thing funny about this situation. I have a four-plus-year-old daughter I have just met because I saw her in the fucking grocery store. A baby's momma I just remembered this morning I fucked—one night might I add—with a goddamn condom on my dick—and she's the fucking daughter of a rival club—their damn princess of all things." I leaned my head back, closed my eyes, and took a deep breath.

Preacher's laugh brought my head back up, and my eyes narrowed when the others joined in. Cruz was the one to gather himself enough to speak.

"Speed, we aren't laughing at you," he wiped his eyes, "we had to be thinking the same thing, though, this moment would have been damn near perfect if Cutter had been here. It brought back the time when you boys spent more time in this office to the point that your asses left prints in the chairs."

I smiled as did the others, remembering, but it was short-lived because I wasn't finished with what the hell was going on and why they hadn't told me.

"It doesn't answer why you haven't told me about my daughter, don't say you had no clue because that little girl looks just like me."

"And did you say two women came into our territory? Who is the other?" Crusher spoke for the first time since entering. We looked toward Stroker again.

"The deputy, she—" Stroker was cut off by Crusher.

"Deputy Bitch is from the Haven MC? Are you shitting me? You didn't think this was important to tell us when we got back or after she and I—" Crusher stopped midsentence, crossed his arms over his chest, and stared at the Prez.

"You and she what, Crusher?" Stroker waited for his question to be answered.

"Nothing, we've been circling around for six fucking months, she rides my ass every chance she gets, and you didn't bother telling me she was from another club. Some of that could have been curtailed with a little knowledge. That's all I was saying." Not by the look, I was reading on his face, but I had my own issues, which brought me to my next question.

"Did you say the VP's daughter? The VP that was planning a fucking coup to take over. Seriously?" Christ, what a huge ass fucking clusterfuck.

"Yes, she and Sami grew up together, she's close with

Sami, and we all know you can't hold the father's stupidity against her. She wasn't helping take the damn club over, nor has she been an issue here." Could have sworn I heard Crusher say under his breath, "Just him."

"We keep getting off subject. Let's get this finished. Speed, Sami and Carly moved here, lived together in a place Wild Bill bought for Sami, and attended college. They didn't come to the club, they didn't hang around the businesses, it wasn't like we sat on them twenty-four/seven, they just lived in our territory. Knew she was pregnant but figured it was by one of the men over in the Haven's club. We never saw the little girl, she applied for the manager's job at Soft Tails. Her knowledge of clubs was a selling point in hiring her, she'd know how to keep her mouth shut. Then the guys apply for positions there, they get hired, and one day the little girl comes in with her because the babysitter was sick. That's when we found out. Tank and the boys who were working saw her, they made the call here and we," his arm swung to include the other dads, "went by with the excuse it was Black Hawk business. We saw her, and I'm surprised Sami didn't pick up on it because I know it shocked the shit out of us. And when that little girl ran up and spoke to us, and lifted her head, Speed, I saw Cutter. If I hadn't known your dad so well, and knew he wouldn't have touched such a young girl, I'd have thought he was the father. We got mad like you that we wasted so much time not knowing the little girl existed and that Sami, coming from a club, knowing what family means to the club and not telling us, yeah, we had our own moment of crazy. Stem saved us from going the fuck off, he'd been the Prospect the day she came to the clubhouse and asked for you about a month or so after you went back to the desert. All she was told was you were gone. So if it helps, she must have come here to tell you.

"Our part, son, when we found out that was the time you were shot and healing, it was a judgment call on our part. We would have notified you if you hadn't come home for good. However, we've taken care of her, she's been protected since the day we found out. Sami doesn't know we know. I don't think she even told Wild Bill. He comes in to visit a few times a year. Usually, by himself, no cut, and only stays a few days. He's never said a word to us, and I'm sure he would. Let's just say the clubs are going to have to come to terms with one another because that little girl ties us, whether we want it or not.

"And let me add, you owe Dare, he's kept this from Shakes. Christ, she will go nuts as if she was really the grandmother, and you boys know that. She's thought of each of you as a son, and she was tough. There were times Dare thought we might kick him out of the club because if she thought we wronged you boys, she was in our shit. We can buy you some time there because that was why we were meeting. Dare and Shakes have a young girl staying with them. Everyone will be told at the next Church that she is their niece and had a few problems at home and will be staying with them for a little while. This part doesn't leave this office, though. Lately, we've been making a few alliances, the newest is the Ops Warriors, they merged two of their clubs and are out of San Diego. They're having a little issue involving the Mexico border, which is part of their territory, and they need to stash her for a time where no one would look for her. Hence, Shakes and Dare's niece." Damn, new changes within Black Hawk every day it seemed. I wasn't done with my own issue yet, one more thing needed to be answered though I thought I already knew this particular answer.

"Why didn't you tell me when I got home?"

Stroker's smile confirmed I was right.

"A test. When I saw her, which you knew evidently I would. You wanted this confrontation. You wanted to see if I would stand up to you, all of you."

"Yes, we knew Cutter had taught you well, but we needed to know you were ready to take his spot. The Enforcer's job of making sure its members follow the rules of the club includes its officers. We needed to see if you would push the envelope." He opened his desk drawer and reached in, "Here, have that on at the next meeting." I caught the patch he'd thrown. "You'll be part of the leadership once the announcement is made at the next full member Church. We hold those once a month. Welcome home, Speed. Now you boys get the fuck out of my office and don't ever barrel in here again like that, or I will kick your asses, personally." Stroker stood along with the other dads as they merged to congratulate me. When I looked at my friends, the smiles on their faces said it all, it was the first step in us taking over Black Hawk.

When I walked out of the office, I had a new perspective and a new outlook. Nothing would stand in my way. I had a daughter to meet. And a woman to get. It would be just a matter of time. The only thing missing was my dad to share it with.

Chapter Twelve

Sami

"So, how was your shift?" I opened the door to let Carly enter.

"Dinner break. Didn't want to go home or to the diner to eat. Oh, pizza. Whatcha got to drink?" She opened the refrigerator, dug in, and pulled out a soda, popping the top while I stuck the pizza in the oven.

"You got time, it will be done in twenty?" I grabbed a drink and joined her at the table.

"Yep, where's shorty?"

"In her room playing. We ran errands and finished with the grocery store."

"Ready to talk about this morning? Were the tears about him?" Carly took a drink and watched me.

"Like I told you. Going to tell me what's with you and

Crusher? Or, as a matter of fact, the whole Black Hawk MC?" My closest friend's eyebrows pushed together, and her eyes flashed.

"Nothing I can't handle, and as far as the club, besides them being arrogant thinking they are all that and then some. I don't think of them. You can't tell me you like the fact they think the sun and the moon set on what they want or that every woman should drop their panties because they enter a room. You and I both were raised around men like that, why would I want to be another notch on someone's bedpost?" Carly crossed her arms over her chest and glared at me.

"Glare all you want. But you know that is total bullshit. Not every one of them is like that. My dad loved my mom, she was everything to him. You saw the good in most the men, just like me. Are you including my dad in that, or what?"

"l love your dad. Living in the club would have sucked if it weren't for him. He moved me here with you and paid my tuition just like yours. However, he is your dad, not mine. You have a parent who loves you and would move heaven and earth for you and Reed. A parent who grieved when he lost his wife. I have a dead mother who died because drugs were more important than her daughter and a dad on the run for being so strung out that he tried to take over the club because he deserved it in his drug-induced mind."

"My dad has never treated you differently because of what your dad tried to do, so don't disrespect him or yourself by making light of him protecting what he considers his family, which includes you. The men in the club may be brash and rough around the edges on a good day, but family is everything, and when they do love, the woman they choose gets their whole heart." I got up, took the pizza out of the oven, grabbed the plates, and moved it to the table. Carly didn't reply until I was on my way to call Ally down for dinner.

"Sami, why don't you take your own advice? The man should know his daughter, and she should have the chance to have a father. I know you don't want her to get hurt, but if he hurts her, that is on him. And I know you, which leads me to believe that it's not all you are worried about because if it were, you wouldn't have protected him by not telling everyone he was your daughter's dad. So I asked myself why would it have made a difference to you, whether he accepted her or not."

I stopped but didn't turn around, "Did you come up with anything since you spend so much time wondering about my choices and not your own?"

"Yes. We've lived here long enough to have learned the story of how the sons of Black Hawk got started. I think you are worried about him thinking you tried to trap him when all you really want is for him to accept her—and most importantly you." I was done listening, I continued on my way to call my daughter to dinner.

Once Ally was in the room, I knew no more would be said about Speed. The three of us ate and laughed at some of the things Ally told us. Mundane things. When dinner was finished, Carly headed back to work, and Ally went to take a bath and get ready for bed.

So when I no longer heard noises from the bathroom, I put the dishcloth down, headed up the stairs, and paused when I reached the doorway. Ally was on the counter, her face pressed close to the mirror, turning her head from side to side, her hands touching her face, her hair.

I walked in quietly, not wanting to scare her. "What are you doing, baby?" She continued to look at herself, only glancing up to acknowledge that I had entered the room.

"Lookin' at my face."

"Well, I can see that, but why?" I smiled when she huffed like it was self-explanatory.

"'Cause he had my face."

"Who had your face? What're you talking about, baby?" I wasn't sure I wanted to know. My stomach clenched, and I rubbed the area.

"The man in the store." Her eyes met mine in the mirror.

"Ally, help me out here. What man and what store?"

"He helped me get the cereal." She sat down on the counter and faced me.

"Yes, you told me about a man helping you, but why does that have you looking in the mirror, sweetie?"

"I told you, he had my face and eyes."

Any other time she'd talk someone's head off. Instead, it was as if I had to pry every drop of information out of her. He'd seen her, and I had no clue how to handle it. Countless times I ran over what I would say when this time came. But as I looked at my daughter, none of it came to me.

"Yes, you did say that. I'm just not understanding

what you think that means."

"We look alike, 'cept he's a boy." Damn it, my time was officially up. Evidently, my daughter and her father had inadvertently met, which led to if she noticed the resemblance, so had he. Awesome.

"What did the man say, baby?"

"Nothing, he gave me the cereal." She scooted down off the counter and looked up at me, lip between her teeth. I'd never felt so sick to my stomach as I had at that moment. I wasn't ready for this. "Did you fix the popcorn?" My breath came back, and my heart started to beat again. I'd never been so thankful for the attention span of a child.

"I will before we start the movie." I picked up the discarded clothes on the floor and followed Ally to her room.

"Can we watch *Frozen*?" Hopeful eyes looked at me, and though we'd watched it a hundred times at least, I couldn't refuse. Not that it would matter what was on, my thoughts would be for the man who ran into the daughter he didn't know about, yet he hadn't bothered to find out why he hadn't been told, so what did that say about him?

"*Frozen* it is." After I had tossed the clothes into the hamper, Ally grabbed the monkey off her bed, and we headed down the stairs. I'd worry tomorrow about how this was going to work out, minimizing the hurt to my daughter was my number one concern, but how did I prepare her for the chance of rejection from a man she'd never met? It was so going to suck.

We sat and watched the movie until Ally had given out

and fallen asleep. I carried her to bed, then grabbed my laptop to work on schedules until I was ready to go to bed or maybe watch some more TV. Anything to take my mind off the changes my life and Ally's was going to go through, sooner rather than later.

Chapter Thirteen

Speed

"Almost five fucking years I've lost. Wish you could see her. Meet her. She's beautiful, just like her mother. It's not like what happened to you with Clarice, I'd thought about the possibility, but it didn't fit. She hadn't known me, and if she'd wanted something you know as well as I, she would have been at the club raising hell. Instead, she went to school, got a job, and from the look of my daughter, she is raising her well." I knelt down with my hands on my knees and smiled for the first time that day.

"I figure I'm going to get a little pushback when I tell the mother she doesn't have much of a choice. Pretty sure Stroker, Cruz, Flyboy, Preacher, and Romeo will get a big kick out of it all. You, too, for that matter. Don't know much about kids, but neither did any of you when you took on parenthood.

"I told you the club was changing, it's a good thing, right? I'll do right by her, just as you did right by me. Grab a beer, hope you enjoy the show." I stood and started back to my bike, I'd put it off long enough. Calmer, I sat on the seat, started my bike, then pulled out.

There I sat on my bike in the driveway and stared at the glow of the light in the window. She was up. Good. The deep breath helped before I dismounted and made my way to the door, and as I stood there with my finger on the bell, the thought that what was behind that door was mine was a heady feeling. It didn't bother me.

The sound of the doorbell followed by footsteps could be heard through the door, and as I watched, I saw the shadow move over the peephole.

A minute went by, and nothing. I pictured her looking at me through the peephole and debating if she should open it or not. Like she had a choice as I stood in place. If she thought I was going to leave, she was nuts.

"You can debate all you want, but I'm not going anywhere. Open the door, Sami. We need to talk. If not, I will talk from here, and I'm sure your neighbors would love it. Up to you. You got one minute to decide." I looked down at my watch and counted the seconds in my head. When I'd hit fifty, the lock turned, and the door was pulled open.

"It's late," was all she said.

"It's eight o'clock." My eyebrow rose, and her hand hit her hip, a little fire entered her eyes.

"If you wanted to talk, you should have come early after you saw her." Hmm… I found it interesting since she hadn't seen me that she knew I'd seen my girl.

"Other things to do before I showed up here." I slid part of my foot in the opening in case she decided to slam the door.

"Figures, you find out you have a daughter, then take care of other things. Wow, she doesn't even know you or you her, and she's taken a back seat to the club." I opened my mouth to speak, but she wasn't done yet.

"Since she seems to have your interest, waiting until tomorrow to see her shouldn't be a hardship." The door started to close, and my foot stopped its progress.

"Think you're getting off that easy, Sami?" I heard the door to the house next door open, and I turned my head at the same time Sami did to watch the older woman step out on her porch.

"Look what you have done. Mrs. Mayson will call the police if you don't leave."

"Who, Sheriff Lance? Maybe your good buddy, Deputy Monroe?"

The older lady stepped off her porch and started across the yard toward us. "Sami, everything okay?" the lady yelled as she got closer.

"He was just leaving," she said, then smirked at me.

"Mrs. Mayson, good to see you. How are you doing, sweetheart?" The look on Sami's face almost made me laugh out loud. Almost.

"Kane Weston?"

"Yes, ma'am."

"Well, get over here, give an old lady a thrill, and hug me." I stepped down off the porch and did just that, lifting her off her feet. She slapped my shoulder and giggled.

"Put me down. Can see the military didn't knock that smoothness out of you boys. Always were full of yourselves." She chuckled as I put her down. I looked back to Sami, who stood in the doorway with her mouth open.

"I'll leave you young people to talk. See you tomorrow, Sami, when you bring Ally over." Mrs. Mayson looked between us and then winked at Sami as if I couldn't see her. All Sami did was nod.

We both didn't speak as we watched Sue walk back to her house and enter, closing the door behind her.

"Going to invite me in to discuss things now, or maybe you prefer to wait until Mr. Sampson across the street comes out to see what's going on. Better yet, I think Mrs. Willis still lives on the corner. Sure she saw me pull up the street. The woman has to be ninety, but she never misses shit." She stepped back, held the door open, and closed it after I walked in. She gave up a little easier than I expected. I'd take it.

"How do you know Sue Mayson?" She'd turned, her green eyes narrowed, and her hands rested on her hips. Her hair was piled upon her head with one of those twisty things women wear. I ran my eyes down her body and back up, she had on shorts and a tank that had seen better days, and I bit the inside of my jaw when her bare foot started tapping the floor. Being near her made me feel more relaxed than I had in years. So, I hadn't been wrong with what I felt with her that one night. We'd get to that later. "Well, you going to stare or answer me?" Damn, she was prettier than I remembered and as cute as my daughter had been in the store.

"Sue was married to my brother, Wolf."

"What? She isn't married. She's lived next door to me since I moved into this house. I think I would know if she were married, she watches my daughter while I am at work."

"Our daughter." Her eyes flashed, but she didn't acknowledge what I said. "Wolf died about twelve years ago. He caught a bad cold, it turned into pneumonia, and he didn't make it."

"Oh, I didn't know…she never said…please can we do this tomorrow? I don't want to wake Ally if our voices rise. We can meet somewhere, maybe in my office, and talk. That would work."

"No." I watched her bottom lick get sucked between her teeth and her nibble on it. But when her tongue came out and ran across her lip as if to wipe away a sting, I found myself wanting to do the same thing to her lips. Which led me to think of her lips kissing their way down my chest until she reached my cock, licking the tip, then wrapping those lips around the head and touching the slit with her tongue. I'd known from her actions she hadn't been very experienced, it hadn't mattered. I'd run my hands in the hair on each side of her head and wrapped the strands around, holding it tight and maneuvered her head how I needed, going deeper with every… Her voice stopped me from having my run down memory lane, and if the tightness in my pants was an indication, it was a good thing.

"Are you going to just stand there? I have to work tomorrow, so either get on with the accusations or anything else you came here for, so you can move on. No sense upsetting Ally if you're not interested in her."

I came for answers and to learn about my daughter, but when she moved her hands from her hips and crossed her arms over her chest, I stepped closer. When she stepped back and sucked that damn lip between her teeth, the air thickened, and tomorrow wouldn't be soon enough.

"Fuck it." I closed the distance, my hands went in her hair, whatever held it on the top of her head shot in the air and landed on the floor while her hair fell in waves down past her shoulders. I tilted her face up, bent down to meet her, and took her mouth, and on her gasp, I pushed my tongue in, her taste slamming into me. I wanted to taste and touch every part of her, remembering our first time was nothing like reliving it. She'd been the only woman in a long line that I'd ever wanted to take my time with. The small moan she released had me pushing her back against the door and taking my time to re-familiarize myself with her body would have to wait as I sucked her lip into my mouth and bit at it. My hands moved to her hips when I felt her body melt into mine. Releasing her lip, I worked my way down until my face pressed into the crook of her neck, and I stopped briefly to lick and suck at the tender spot. Her hands were on my shoulders, holding on while I moved over her shoulder, sliding the tank material off her shoulder as I continued the path until the strap of her top slipped down her arm.

I worked my thigh between her legs, and when she spread so I could push between them, the heat from her center radiated through the material of my jeans to heat my skin. The need to feel her heat wrapped around my cock was almost more than I could take.

Holding her in place with one hand on her shoulder, my other hand tore at the snap of her shorts, moving around her waist, pushing the material of her shorts and panties over her hips as they gave way. I pulled back long enough to push them to the floor before I grabbed her, turned her to face the door, and pulled her hips to me. One arm wrapped around her as I splayed my hand over her mound, my middle finger easily sliding through to rest on her clit and I put pressure on the nub until she pushed back of her own accord. My other hand fought to release my cock, once in hand, I ran it through her slickened folds, aligning it to her opening, then paused.

"Say it," I gritted through my teeth. I needed to hear the words, her actions were not enough. I pushed into her, the tip of my dick barely entering, "Goddammit, Sami, say the words, and I'll put both of us out of misery." One of the hands she'd had palm against the door she brought down, placed it over mine on her mound, and pressed down, using both our hands to rub her clit.

Her body shivered, and she groaned, "Fuck me. Please," was all I needed to hear. I thrust into her to the hilt, her gasped cry was from pleasure since the hand on mine began to pick up the pace as she moved it back and forth over her clit. Pulling out and slamming back in with a force that had her lifted till she was stretched up on her toes.

We reached the end together, the walls of her pussy milking me as my release filled her. Her forehead leaned on the door as mine rested on her shoulder, each of us needing a minute to catch our breath. I was the first to recover as I turned her, placed my shoulder on her stomach, and lifted her bent over my shoulder, her hand grabbing the waist of my pants to either keep them from falling or to hold herself from bouncing as I started up the stairs.

"You can't just come in here and—" The smack to her ass cut her off in the middle of what I presumed to be the beginning of some tirade.

"Hush, you'll wake my daughter up," I whispered as we reached the top.

"My daughter. Now put me down." She wiggled, and I tightened my grip.

"Our daughter, which room." I moved down the hall.

"You aren't staying here; you need to leave." My free hand moved between her legs and pushed a finger in.

"What, room?" I asked as I slid the finger in and out, her pussy readying again as it tried to suck the digit deep.

"The last one," came out breathlessly as she shifted to meet the movement of my finger. Entering the room, I pushed the door closed with my foot and walked to the bed, tossing her on it. My clothes were removed before she even stopped bouncing.

I moved toward the bed and her eyes locked with mine, the green bright and shining with desire, her skin pink from exertion, a spot on her forehead red where her head must have banged the door as I pounded into her. I should leave, I knew it, it's what a gentleman would do, but I was far from that.

"I remember you being feisty, I loved it. Let's see if I can get you to orgasm as many times as I did that night." Her eyes rounded, and her tongue licked her lips as I pumped my cock, "Later, I'll be glad to let you suck my cock, baby, but right now, I need it to make up the time I've lost in your pussy."

She didn't have time to respond before I was on the bed and she was under me. When I surged into her, I had to push the feeling of home out of my mind, so I began to move.

Chapter Fourteen

Sami

The heat from the sun shining through the window had me stretching my body out. The twinge in my lower region was what brought my eyes open as I recalled why. Without rolling over, I slid my hand to the other side of the mattress, only touching cool sheets. It seemed he'd been gone for a while, and I hadn't even heard him leave.

We talked in between the bouts of sex. I didn't know where the man found the energy and stamina, and I sure as hell wasn't going to complain. He'd known more about me than I had of him. That was probably more from the officers of Black Hawk. No doubt they knew plenty about me, but I never gave them credit for figuring out who fathered Ally.

As he held me, I'd caught myself tracing his tattoos like I'd done our first time together, he had a lot, but the work was beautifully done, and it gave me something to do while we talked. He told me about him and the other sons of Black Hawk, how they came to be, how close they were because of it. It felt like he was trying to give me pieces of him as if to let me know him. He talked of his dad and their relationship, and I told him of mine with my dad. We skipped over the part about my father being Haven's president. I found it odd that we were so relaxed with each, it was easy to want more with him, but I knew how men were in the clubs. Some had kids with women, they just didn't see the need to be tied down with it, so I was under no delusion that this was to be more than what it was—lust and convenience of the parties involved.

It was hard not to hate myself for being weak where this man was concerned, my only excuse was I lost all rationality when he touched me. Ugh, he confused me, and I didn't have time for it.

We'd talk about Ally later, he said. Well, he would have to come to me, I had a job and things to do. I threw the blankets off and got up to walk to the bathroom, and that's when I heard the soft peals of laughter—one deeper than the other—shit.

After dashing into the bathroom, then around the room to find and put on clothes, I headed downstairs. When I passed the front door, I noticed no clothes lying on the floor, thank God. Hitting the kitchen, the sight stopped me in my tracks.

Speed stood in front of the stove while Ally stood in a chair beside him, their backs to me. I stood there for a moment, mesmerized by the picture they made. Their black hair shined from the light in the room, and that's when I noticed Ally's hair was up in a ponytail, and she was already dressed. Another facet of the man, he'd fixed a little girl's hair. I shook my head, yes, it would be easy to want it all with him. Too fast, who falls for a man that you've briefly been around twice, each time revolving around sex? Explosive sex, but still.

"Can I put more in?"

"Hold up a minute, I got to get the other off the griddle first." I watched him slide the pancake onto a plate, then move the pan over in front of Ally so she could put more batter on it before replacing it on the heated burner.

"Morning." I watched as their heads turned, and two sets of identical eyes looked at me.

Ally jumped from the chair and ran to me, "Hey, Momma, we're making breakfast." I leaned down and hugged her, and once lose she went back to get on her chair.

"I can see that, baby."

"Come here." The way he said it had me moving toward him.

"Did you need me to take over the stove?" He was probably uncomfortable being in my kitchen.

"Nope, wanted to do this." Before I knew what he was going to do, he leaned in and kissed my forehead, "Morning." He turned back to the stove, plated another pancake, and let Ally add more batter while I stood there blinking and wondered if I was still in my bed dreaming.

"Momma, you going to eat too? I'm helpin' cook."

"Hmm…sure." Speed winked at me, and I turned, grabbed a cup of coffee, then got plates and silverware to set the table. Maybe it was an alternate universe.

It wasn't long, and the three of us were seated at the table having breakfast like a family. My daughter talked and giggled as though a strange man sat at our table daily. Speed interacting with her as though they'd done it a thousand times as I sat there and watched. Then I got annoyed as I thought about how he steamrolled over me, using sex whenever I tried to discuss anything he didn't want to talk about.

"You working today?" I glanced at him when he spoke.

"Yes, in a few hours, actually. Don't you have to be somewhere?" Yeah, it sounded a little snotty. And when he smirked, my annoyance increased.

"Sure do, and I will get to it after I finish eating. Woke hungry for some reason this morning." He had the gall to wink at me and go back to shoveling food into his mouth.

Deciding to ignore him, "You got dressed and everything this morning already, Ally?"

"Uh huh, I got up, and Speed came out of your room. He said you was still sleeping and that if I went and got dressed, I could help him fix breakfast for you."

"Well, thank you, baby. It's a great breakfast." I looked at Speed, and he shrugged.

"I ran into Ally after I'd put your laundry in your room that was left by the front door last night."

"Oh."

"Yeah, oh," he chuckled.

"He fixed my hair too." I looked at her and back to Speed.

"What? Did you want her in front of the stove with her hair flying everywhere?"

"No. Feel free to go when you are done, I'll clean up the kitchen since you cooked."

"You coming back today, Speed?"

"Ally, Speed probably has stuff to do." I pointedly looked at him, and he sat back and then crossed his arms over his chest.

"We'll see. Your mother and I have things to talk about." Yes, we did, like how he acted like he had every right to walk in and take over my life because we once slept together over five years ago and shared a kid. Then he enters my home, and when we should have been hashing things out, he kisses me, and before I can think, we are having sex up against the door. It also didn't escape me that, thank God, Ally slept like the dead, considering she was in her bed while her mother was slutting it up. It was mutual sex, but how was I supposed to think when he was touching me and kissing me, for fuck's sake?

"Not today, Ally. I don't get off till late."

"'K. Maybe tomorrow you can come over?" Then she turned to me. "Can I watch TV until you get ready?"

"Yes, you can." We watched her jump down and take off for the living room, and he didn't wait long after the sound of the TV hit our ears.

"Before you start, I was going to get out of here

before she woke," he got up and put his plate in the sink, "but I walked into her in the hall. Figured the best thing was to act as normal as possible."

"Thank you, I do appreciate that and breakfast, but…"

"I wanted to tell her, but I also didn't want to freak her out. I want to get to know my daughter, Sami. You won't keep me from her." He looked at his watch. "I gotta be going, meeting the guys. I'll tell her bye on my way out."

"I think it best if we take it slow with her, then if you stick, we can tell her, and if not, well, she won't get hurt." He smiled when I looked up at him. "What the hell are you smiling at."

"She won't get hurt, Sami, and neither will you. I'm not going anywhere. Now come and kiss me goodbye."

"I concede on telling her about you, Speed, but that doesn't have anything to do with me. We had sex, and it was good. I don't need to be part of the equation and don't want you to feel that you have to be. I won't be used so that you can spend time with our daughter. The convenient pussy when you need to be laid." I stood. "I'll walk you out. I have to get ready myself."

"Fair enough." He followed me down the hall to the front door. I opened it up for him. "Later, Ally."

"Bye, Speed."

He walked through the door and pulled me out with him as he closed the door behind us. "What are you doing? You can't just—" He leaned and kissed me. "You can't—" He did it again. This time when he stood in front of me, I just stared at him and that damn smirk on his face.

"Good, you catch on fast." He held up a finger to stop me from speaking. "Now listen. I'm going to spend time with my daughter, and I'm going to spend time with you. This is how this is going to work. I'll give you time to get used to this idea because it is going to happen. You and Ally, my house, you in my bed. I want her to be on the Black Hawk compound. Uh uh, don't speak, I'm not done. I want you there too, if you need to justify it as me needing convenient pussy, go with that, but know you have a week to get used to the idea, I'll give that to you. I'd rather you come on your own but don't get me wrong—you will come, even if I have to move your stuff myself." The kiss was hard and rough this time as he took my mouth, stepped back, turned, and mounted his bike. I hadn't moved as he drove away, I stood there and watched until his bike disappeared before going into the house. What the fuck just happened?

"I know you don't have time to sit, but I can see the questions you have for me in your eyes. No, I didn't know who the father was when I first started babysitting Ally when you were in class or working at the diner. You and Carly moved in, and I was just glad to have respectful young people next door who would give an old lady the time of day.

"Then you had Ally, and you needed help with her, that's it all was in the beginning, helping a person in need. Now, I think of you and that little girl as family. Wolf and I couldn't have children, and over these few years, I consider you and Carly, though she is a tough bird to crack, as daughters." I had no words, Ally was in the living room with the TV on and playing. I'd dropped her off so I could go to work. Did I want to ask questions? Sure, but I figured I would get into those when I picked my daughter up later. Now with Sue's words, I wanted to cry. She had been a lifesaver over the years here, and I couldn't be mad at her for not telling me before of her ties to Black Hawk.

"I had an idea who the father was as Ally grew into her features and those eyes of hers, well they're recognizable because I've only seen two men with those eyes, not to mention that girl has the hair color and facial features of those men too. Speed looks like his daddy, and Ally looks like both of them. It wouldn't take five seconds for anyone who knew the men and saw Ally to make the connection. So I wasn't shocked when Stroker and the others called and asked me to keep an eye on you and let them know if there was anything you or she needed.

"You were raised in a club, Sami. You know family is family." Yes, I understood how men in the MC life operated, didn't have to be happy about it, but I understood.

"Ugh, I'd love to sit down and discuss everything, but I've got to get to work. I don't really know him. I was expecting to be accused of intentionally getting pregnant, but he never asked about that. I'm so confused with him, and I don't have the time to analyze any of it." I headed back through the house, hugged my daughter bye, and walked outside with Sue not far behind.

She followed me to my car, and when I sat before

closing the car door, she said, "One thing to think about when you do get the time is those men go after what they want, and they usually get it." She turned and went back into the house. I closed the door and headed to Soft Tails. Didn't need to think about Sue's words, I knew the men always got what they wanted—I just didn't want Ally and me to be the casualties when Speed decided he wanted something else.

The sound of voices in the hall let me know it was close to the time for the club to open as I heard a few girls pass by my office door. I needed to get up and check to ensure everyone who was on the schedule to work had shown up.

The first stop was the dressing room of the strippers. I walked in to find Candie, Syn, and Lindy putting their personal things away.

"You're such a slut, girl." Candie was talking when I walked in. "Hey, boss lady, come on in and take a load off. Lindy was sharing her weekend slut-tales with us."

"Well, by all means, don't let me stop you." I shook my head. It amazed me how these women showed no shame in talking about who or what they did. There were times I wished I could be that unguarded.

"So you have had sex with all six of them? Damn, girl, when you came out of the room, you had the smile of someone who won the lottery and the walk of a woman whose ass had been ridden hard and was feeling the aftereffects. Syn, you really need to come to the Black Hawk clubhouse one weekend."

"Not me, I don't have the time nor the inclination to ride a half dozen dicks or suck as many off. My off time is too important." Syn started undressing, getting ready for her set since she was due up first. Syn was here with Candie and Babs when I took over, but I realized she was also the one I knew less about. She didn't share the private part of her life.

"Hon, it's less expensive than the price of batteries." We all chuckled.

"True on all accounts, Candie. I got to have all six of the sons of Black Hawk, though give me some credit, I didn't have all their dicks up my ass or pussy, so I can't say how each of them is in that department. However, I did have the dicks, it just happened I only got to blow four of them." I couldn't say a word, I stood there and watched Lindy as she flicked her hair off her shoulder as if she'd done what no woman had, at least to me and my limited experience with banging six at one time. Damn, I'd only fucked two men in my life, and one of them was evidently a couple of days after he had his cock in someone else.

"Devil and Flirt were the riders, the others got lip action. But I do know the six are holding big, thick, and long cocks that any woman would love, and the added bonus is they know how to use them. Now that I've had each, I'll be going back for seconds, thirds, etc. Next time though, I think I'd like to do the riding on the cocks, it would be like being a mare getting fucked by a few stallions, one right after the other. And I have no problem with walking a little stiff for a couple of days."

"Nice analogy, Lindy." Syn shook her head while I

stood there and got pissed, which I would evaluate later with everything else that had to do with Speed.

"Did you girls know too that Speed is Ally's dad?" It was out of my mouth before I knew what I'd said. Three sets of eyes stared at me, but Lindy was the only one with their chin on the floor. Totally caught her off guard, but Candie and Syn not so much, and the back and forth on their feet as they dropped their eyes to the floor, told me I nailed it with them. "How long?"

"Sorry, Sami. I didn't know. Excuse me," Lindy said when she passed me and headed out the dressing room door.

"Well?" I continued to stare at Candie and Syn.

"The first time you brought her in, and we saw her," Candie whispered, and Syn shook her head in agreement.

"Why did you not say anything or ask? Have you slept with him too, Candie?" Not sure I wanted the answer to that.

"No, and I'm not saying I wouldn't have, but I had just started at Soft Tails right before you came to town. They were all gone to the military and only came home every so often. It never worked out that I got to fuck either of them." I only shook my head in acknowledgment, I didn't want to hurt her feelings, she'd been the first person Carly and I had met when we moved here, and I liked her too.

"Syn?"

"Not me, girl. The only party I went to was when we took you out there. As I said, don't really have time for all that. I called a cab and left after you were hauled off, and Candie took off with someone else." We'd never talked about that night, I'd just assumed they'd partied at the clubhouse on the weekends. Now I was pissed that I seemed to be a shitty friend on top of everything else.

"Still doesn't answer why you didn't say anything?"

"Figured you'd tell if you wanted us to know." I turned from Candie to Syn.

"Same with me, Sami. Sorry." I needed to go to my office and sit at my desk until time to go home.

"Almost time to open, I'll be in my office." I hightailed it the fuck out of there.

"You got it, boss," was the last thing they both yelled as I closed the dressing room door behind me. It was going to be a long day and evening since I was ready to go home.

Chapter Fifteen

Speed

It never failed to amaze me every time I rode up to the clubhouse. The log cabin was huge and had served as a lodge back before the dads had bought it for the club, the place was spacious, and they'd renovated the inside for their needs. It had twelve individual cabins, which each of the originals had taken one and lived in. Those, too, had been renovated to suit the men. They were still referred to as cabins though they were as big as some people's homes. The one I'd shared with my dad had four bedrooms, one set up as an office, a kitchen, a living room, and three bathrooms. I'd asked once why we had such a big house, and Cutter had told me that after living in the barracks and small apartments during his military career, he'd told himself that if he ever owned a home, it would be open and spacious. Considering the other ones that sat around ours, they too were large.

One of the stories Roscoe loved to tell was how the dads bought the place off him and gave him a home and a reason to live after losing his wife the year before they'd come to town. That let him become a member when they saw the Harley in the shed while checking out the property, and he'd told them it was his. He and his wife had run the lodge; after she died, he'd lost interest and didn't want to do it alone. He now lived in one of the other six cabins across the way next door to Shakes and Dare.

After I went home and took a shower when I got back from Sami's, I walked to the clubhouse, went in the back door, and I saw Daisy standing over the stove cooking.

"Hey, sugar, lookin' good." She swung around and squealed. First time I'd seen her since I got back.

"Speed, good to have you home. Sorry I missed you when you got in. I'd left that morning to go over to my sister's, she's been down ill." Daisy hugged me and went back to cooking, no doubt fixing something for any of the men who were hanging around.

"How's your sister doing, Daisy?" Her sister lived a couple of hours away from the club and had made it known that she hadn't cared for her sister's lifestyle choice.

"Better, same bitchy ass. I do her a favor and still have to listen to that same crap I did thirty years ago. My consolation was, she's younger but has more wrinkles than one of those Shar Pei dogs." I would give Daisy that, she'd taken care of herself over the years.

"Seen the others come through here?"

"If you're talking the younger bunch, no. Stroker and the others are in his office, and a few members are roving around here somewhere." She circled her hand in the air to include the whole place.

"Thanks, darlin'. Catch you later." I didn't wait for a reply as I headed through the clubhouse. When I reached the office, I knocked.

"Open," was yelled, and I walked in to find the officers sitting around.

"Need something, Speed?" Stroker raised his head from the papers in front of him to look at me while the others saluted their hello.

"Just checking in to see if you need anything."

"Nope, pretty quiet today. Umm…heard you didn't come home last night. Taking you handled a little personal business," Romeo smirked.

"Bet he took care of than one piece of business, considering he walked in here all lose-hipped," Flyboy laughed, and the others joined in.

"Looks like I'm going to be the most mature one in this group now." All that had done was make them laugh louder.

"Don't dodge, boy. We going to have a little one running around here soon or what?" Preacher stopped laughing, and his eyebrow cocked at me.

"Better yet, is an ol' lady going to be moving in your place?" Cruz hit his thigh, and they all laughed again. Fuckers thought they were so damn funny. They'd spent their entire lives avoiding getting tied down.

"Let's just say I'm not running." The door opened, and my friends walked in. "I'm done sticking my dick in any hole just because they're available."

"Brother, are you sick? You haven't been back a week yet. Taking over the Enforcer job, there will be many women wanting to congratulate you with a wet, wild ride." Flirt had always been a dog.

"Leaves more for you guys." I'd stepped in just to tell them of a few changes that would be coming, not to discuss feelings and shit.

"Damn straight it does. We'll take it too, but are you sure?" Jag was always serious.

"I'm sure. Surer than I've been in a long while."

"Then, man, we'll be happy for you." Coast walked up to me and slapped my back. I noticed Crusher hadn't spoken, so I turned toward him.

"Don't have nothing to say?"

"I do," Devil spoke up, "One pussy for the rest of your life. You sure a bullet didn't graze your head when your group got hit?"

"No, but what I do know, I got a daughter whose life I want to be a part of."

"Okay, understand that but, Speed, you don't have to take the mother on to do that," Stroker spoke, and Crusher still hadn't said a word.

"What's your problem, man?" I asked him. He looked at each man in the room until his eyes landed back on me.

"Does the little girl know you're her dad?"

"Not yet, she will be here soon, Crusher, you know

me?"

"Good." His arm went out, and he motioned to others, "Unlike this bunch, I understand what you're feeling. When should we expect them to be moving here, because I know you well when you set your mind to something." He had me smiling then as I remembered the dazed look on Sami's face that morning when I'd said it to her.

"A week."

"Son, not that I don't believe you will get what you want, but you know her dad may not agree with you, regardless of what she does." I'd thought of that already, and I'd take whatever he dished out, then he'd better get the fuck over it.

"I'll face that shit when it comes." I rubbed my neck when smiles spread on the dads' faces. "And it will be coming soon."

"Never was slow on the draw, boy. We were here because I received a call from Wild Bill. He was clearing it with us to come to visit Sami, his granddaughter, and Carly. And hey, you get a twofer, her brother, Reed, is coming too. He's an Enforcer for the Haven." Stroker smiled, and his lips twitched. The others didn't refrain from letting out their laughter.

"Fucking great." Nothing like meeting the whole family.

"Now get out and go get that business you boys are starting ready to go." We took the hint and cleared out.

Once we reached the garage behind my place and started working on what we needed to get up and running, I was able to put Sami and the situation out of my mind.

"When are the parts due in for your dad's bike?" Jag asked as he finished writing up the order for the parts we needed to have on hand to start building the first custom bike. A rich lawyer from Arizona with more money than he needed.

"Day after tomorrow, Chuck's going to drive them out and drop them off for me. My stuff that I had shipped from the military will be here too. I'll buy the beer and pizza if you guys can stop over to help me sort the shit out, maybe work on getting a routine down, starting with Dad's bike."

"Works for me." Flirt finished, straightening the shelves with the different cans of paint, cleaners, and solvents needed.

"Me too," Devil said, followed by the same from Coast and Jag. Crusher was outside wiping off the dust from some of the equipment.

"I'll check with Crush to see if he's in." I stepped outside to check and found Crusher just standing there, rag in hand, staring off. "You okay, man?" He turned at my voice.

"Yeah, just about done, then we can move the stuff back in." He bent back down and continued with his job.

"What were you doing, brother? You have been a little quiet today." For him, he had. Crusher was usually very vocal. He continued wiping down the equipment, his brows furrowed, so I knew he was thinking.

"You're really going to do this?"

"Yep." I knew he was done.

"She pushes the bad away of what we've seen? Brings peace?" He was talking about Sami.

"Yeah, she does."

"I thought so." He looked up at me then, "Happy for you, brother. Hope to have it one day myself."

"Got someone in mind?"

"We'll see. Maybe."

"Need to talk about it?"

"No." He returned to work, and I went back to the garage to tell the others we were on. Crusher would talk when ready.

By the time we finished, it was late. Shakes, Dare, and their *niece* stopped by, Shakes was in her element, but at least the guys and I hadn't had to stop and cook anything, Dare had put the lasagna Shakes had made on the kitchen counter before they came into the garage. The woman could cook, and every one of us was grateful for the meal.

After we had eaten, the others went home, and I sat in my living room and tried to watch some TV. Instead, I was restless, so a ride on my bike would do the trick, the night air felt good blowing on my face. I found myself driving past Soft Tails and looking for Sami's car, it was gone, which then led me to where I sat now. Down the street from her house, far enough away she couldn't see me from any of her windows, but close enough I could see the lights on through the blinds, so I knew she was still up. Ally should be in bed since it was late. What would she do if I came to her door again? I wouldn't, though, I'd give her tonight to absorb everything, then tomorrow I talked the others into going to the club. If she thought I would stay out of her way until the week was up, she wasn't as smart as I thought. I could be a prick, but at the end of the day, I'd be her prick, starting in one week. I smiled inwardly and started my bike. One more stop, and then I'd be tired enough to sleep. At least, I hoped so.

"Out for a ride and thought I'd stop by. Not looking forward to going to the house alone, but I'll survive for the next few days. Parts are due in for your bike, the guys are going to help me restore it. We got all the things in place to start Sons of Black Hawk Custom Bikes, even the first order.

"I got to spend the morning with my daughter today. You'd love her, Dad, she's sweet with a little meanness built in. And Sami, well, I know you and the others never wanted to take ol' ladies, maybe because you never found the right one, I don't know. All I know is when Sami touches me, every bad thing I've seen or done goes away, and it's just her. My mind rests when she's lying next to me, and when I look into her eyes, I see the good this world has to offer. I'm going to build a life with her and my daughter.

"I best get back, I won't sleep as peacefully tonight, but maybe if I think of Sami and Ally in the house soon, I'll get a couple of hours. Love ya, Dad, and miss ya."

Chapter Sixteen

Speed

We finished eating at the diner and were heading back to my house to sort the parts that were dropped off this morning to begin work on my dad's bike when I saw Ally walking hand in hand with the deputy. I pulled over with my brothers behind me and turned off the bike as they did the same with theirs.

"Aunt Carly, it's Speed! Hi, Speed!" I chuckled, and so did the guys at her pulling the deputy with one hand and waving at us with her free hand.

"Hey, darlin'. What are you up to?" I watched her look over the bikes before she answered. The girl knew what was important already, and she didn't know it.

"Aunt Carly picked me up from school today and took me to the park. We're going to the bakery now so I can get a cupcake. They're my favorite." When she finished, I looked at the others, and they had smirks on their faces. The girl could talk.

"That so. Where's your momma at?" The deputy stood there quietly, which didn't go unnoticed, but I did catch her eyes going from me to Crusher, who was right beside me.

"Momma is cleaning 'cause Papa is coming this weekend, and she won't have any time to do it before he gets here. At least that's what she says. When you gonna have a sleepover with Momma again, so we can make pancakes again for breakfast." The deputy barely contained her laughter, but she did turn away, the guys not so much as their loud laughter had people walking down the street turning and looking at them.

"Soon, darlin', soon." It didn't slow her down, but when she turned her attention to the guys, I got to laugh.

"Who are you? Are you Speed's friends? You can come with him and have a sleepover at my house too. I like bikes. I want ones, but Momma said I had to get older. Aunt Carly has a bike. I like your bikes. When I get older, can I ride them? Benji said I can't have a bike 'cause only boys can. Aunt Carly said Benji is a little bastard, which is bad. You don't say bad words, do you? I punched Benji in the nose 'cause he said I couldn't go to the school the day the daddies got to come 'cause I don't have one." I thought she was done, but she was only catching her breath, and as she stepped closer while she talked, I lifted her and sat her in front of me on my bike. She looked back at me and smiled but never missed a beat. Her Aunt Carly was chuckling, and I was sure it had to do with the looks on my brothers' faces, the look that said, "What the fuck."

"This is a pretty bike. I want one just like it. Why do your handle thingies stick up further than everyone else's?" That was geared toward Flirt, but she didn't need him to answer. "Will you teach me to ride? Then when I get big, I can ride with you. Do you have daddies? Speed's daddy is gone, which is code for dead 'cause I heard my momma say that people shouldn't tell kids someone died. Why don't they want to tell us? I watched an ant die when the boy at the park held a glass over it. Did you ever hold a glass over an ant and watch it die?" When she stopped to take a breath this time, Carly cut in.

"Shortcake, I think you made their ears bleed enough. Let's go see Bailey at the bakery." I set Ally back on the ground, and she took Carly's hand. "Gentlemen, I use that term loosely due to little ears, have a good one."

"Bye, darlin'. Tell your momma I will see her later."

"'K, Speed."

"Deputy," Crusher spoke for the first time but then again, no one got a chance to talk when Ally started.

"Mr. Davis. Come on, shortstop." Ally giggled, and they turned and started to walk away.

"You got a smart mouth, I like that. You always a hardass?" I looked at Crusher, he was really going to provoke the deputy. The "that's a bad word" from Ally had us laughing at Crusher, but it didn't faze him or the deputy.

"No, only to assholes who think women should fall at

their feet because they deem it." Ally smiled up at the deputy, and once again, we heard, "that's a bad word." I figured one day at the clubhouse, around the members, and we'd hear that a good thousand times.

"Know what I like more than seeing you walking toward me, Deputy?" She stopped at the door of the bakery and looked back at him.

"What?"

"Walking away, Deputy." I couldn't believe I heard my brother use that lame-ass line, and the "Jesus" that echoed from the others made me smile.

She laughed, shook her head, and Ally waved at us, then they walked into the bakery. I looked at Crusher, "Seriously, walking away, what the hell is wrong with you?"

"I was going to say watching her ass as she walked away, but I didn't want to get 'that's a bad word' said to me again."

"She's beautiful, Speed."

"Thanks, Jag."

"I agree, brother, but damn she can talk. Her first time at the clubhouse. I am videoing that shit. She's going to have every damn one of the men wrapped around her finger as soon as she starts talking."

"That's all true, Flirt."

"Man, she's got a bite to her too. She punched a kid. Gotta love that."

"Yeah, Devil, she does. Makes for quite the package."

"I want to know who that Benji kid belongs to."

"Me too, Coast." I smiled, the Enforcer showing in

him too.

"Going to build that bike, Speed?" Crusher grinned, and I grinned back, and we all burst out laughing.

"Well, let's head back. Get some work done, and I will buy the first round tonight at Soft Tails."

With that, we started our bikes and headed out.

Sami

"Momma, I saw Speed and his friends!" I heard no sooner than the door opened. I walked out of the kitchen to greet my daughter and Carly, who wore a huge ass smile.

"Did you? Where did you run into him, baby?"

"At the bakery. He said he'd see ya soon. Did you clean for Papa and Uncle Reed?"

"Yes. Why don't you go upstairs and play a little before you have to go to Mrs. Mayson's house and I have to go to work." Ally ran up the stairs, and I looked at the now smirking Carly.

"You seem in a good mood today?"

"Sure am, but I would think you would be in a better mood since you're the one who got to have a sleepover the other night."

Well, shit.

"Sami, relax. I'm not going to go off because you slept with Ally's dad or because he spent time with her. My issues are my issues. I don't want you hurt, that's all, but I have to say, seeing them together and the way he looked at her and listened. How all of them listened to her, though I admit the 'my ears are bleeding looks' were amusing to me, they already have accepted her. And I will support any decision you make in regards to him." Her words only made me love her more.

I wasn't going to share what I had found out about him with her, not when she was letting her misgivings go a little. I saw the old Carly showing through. The one before we moved here because her dad had pulled his shit. No way was I going to tamper with that.

"We'll see. Are you staying a while?" She hadn't moved from the door.

"No, going home to catch a little sleep. Switched a couple of shifts so I could have some time to spend with your dad when he comes."

"Don't forget Reed is coming too."

"Who could forget that." She turned and opened the door. "I won't see you till Saturday. And by the way, Speed did say to tell you he would see you later. Don't do anything I wouldn't do." She walked out and then yelled over her shoulder, "Oh, I forgot, you already have."

"Bitch."

"You know it." She laughed and got in her truck, and drove off.

I wanted to tell her I wasn't going to be doing anything because I had no plans to be used. Sharing Ally, fine, but I had no intention of being part of the deal. I didn't care that I heard a motorcycle and looked out the window to see him driving by last night. And I had no intention of sharing the fact I thought it was sweet when I saw him at the cemetery standing in front of a headstone, which I figured was his dad's, right after he came back as I was driving home that day. Nope, not sharing any of that. Satisfied, I closed the door, a little nap sounded good before I had to go to work. Maybe Ally would lie down too.

Chapter Seventeen

Speed

Soft Tails was busy when we parked our bikes and headed in. Tank and Rock were talking at the door when we entered.

"Brothers," they both said at the same time when they saw us.

"Hey, guys. Club's busy tonight. How are you doing?"

"Good, Speed. You going to do right by our girls?" My eyebrow went up, and Crusher slapped my back.

"News sure does travel fast through the club these days." Everyone chuckled at Crusher's observation.

"Glad you men have been watching after them, but I think you meant my girls, Tank."

The smile split his face, and he stuck out his hand, "She's in her office." I took it for what it was meant for, brothers looking out for each other and their families.

We walked through to find a table, and some of the members I hadn't seen since Church saluted us with their beers as we walked by.

"Hey, Speed." Roscoe had stopped me before I'd gotten halfway across the floor. He was sitting with a few of the club's older members.

I slapped him on the back, "How's life treating you, Roscoe?"

"Good, Speed. You going to do right by my girl?" Christ, on the one hand, I was glad to see my brothers cared, but this 'my girl and our girls' was going to get old, I just knew it.

"Roscoe, glad you care about her, but that would be 'my girl,' not yours." The men sitting at the table with him snickered. And Roscoe winked.

"That's what I wanted to hear." I slapped his back again and started to the empty table in the back, it would give me a great view of the whole club, and I would see Sami whenever she walked through.

"Man, those two are going to turn this club upside down. I've never seen any of them this taken with anyone." I was almost certain Flirt was right.

I waved them ahead of me and pointed to the table that was empty, "You guys go sit and order, I'm going to go ahead and make my rounds to stop this mine and our shit." I started for the bar, and their laughter followed me. Fuckers.

'Our girls' were repeated by Stem and Frankie, then I pushed through the door to the kitchen and saw Perry at the sink washing a few dishes. When he heard the door open, he turned.

"Speed, good to see you, son. You claiming my girls?" What the fuck? Did every man who came in contact with those two fall or what? I was going to have a mile-long list of asses to kick, *MY* girls had lived here for a while.

"Perry, good to see you. I have a list of asses to kick, don't make me add you to it. I'm going out to have a beer or two with my friends, maybe get to see *MY* girl while she works."

"Sucked you in already, have they?" He chuckled and stuck out his hand. I laughed and took his hand to shake.

"One hundred percent." Perry turned back to his dishes, and I walked out to join my friends.

We'd sat at the table for about an hour before she walked out of the office, and I watched her make her rounds to her people. As I watched her, I didn't have to say anything to know I was going to be a lucky bastard when she accepted that she was mine. Then I thought of Ally, 'that's a bad word' deal.

"What the hell you smiling at, brother?" Devil nudged me, then followed the direction I was looking.

"Seriously, man, you are a goner." Hell, no sense in lying.

"I know, and I'm man enough to admit it." He shook his head.

Lindy stopped by to see if we were ready for another round, then went to the bar to fill our order. I watched Sami go back into the kitchen, and by the time she came out,

Lindy was on her way back to our table. She'd just stepped between me and Flirt to set the beers down when Sami looked over and saw me. She continued to walk through, only she avoided our table and was at the other side talking with Roscoe.

Huh, what the hell, she had smiles and laughs for him, then when she looked back over toward me, the smile went away. Oh hell, something was off. She finally walked toward me as Lindy walked off.

"Everyone doing okay tonight?" The guys acknowledged it was going great, but they didn't turn from watching Syn start her routine.

"Come here." I watched her eyes flash as she looked at me.

"I don't think so. Have a good evening." She went to walk past, and I stopped her with my hand on her arm. She looked down at it and then back to me.

"Excuse me, could you remove your hand?" Oh yeah, something was up, I'd find out, but I wasn't going to make a scene so the brothers could watch.

"Sure, you're working, I get it."

She rolled her eyes and walked off. She'd be lucky I didn't spank her ass when I got to her house tonight.

"Wow, you sure the 'my woman' is understood by her? Because if she is like that in bed—you'd have to fuck her with long johns on.

"Shut up, Coast." My brows pulled together as I watched her head back into her office. I was going to see what the fuck was going on and stop it before it got any worse. I pushed back my chair and started for her office. Yeah, we were going to have a chat.

Sami

He didn't knock. He just walked right in and shut the door behind him. My expression had to be one of shock when I heard the lock slide into place. His facial expression was one of a man who was pissed. When his mouth opened, I was more than ready.

"Want to tell me what crawled up your ass?"

"No, go see if Lindy will talk with you." He had no clue what I was talking about from the look he was returning.

"Watch the attitude, darlin'. Don't want to turn that soft pale ass bright red."

"Sure, you would have to be in my bed to do that. You won't be, so it's really no concern of mine."

"Ah, I don't think you understand what is going to happen."

"I understand perfectly. But Lindy would probably accept it, maybe even reciprocate with a blowjob." I flipped my hair over my shoulder.

"Heard about that, did you?" He acted as if that was acceptable.

"Why yes, inadvertently, but I'm not going to make you give up any play toys. I just am not going to be one. That's all." Hopefully, that would get him out of the office.

"Hmm… I see. You want me to leave, and I will, but it will be after I show you something." He didn't have a right, but he was pissed now. Fucking good for him.

When he should have been headed for the door, he was stalking toward me as if I was his prey. If I went by the promise that was shining in his eyes, I should be scared. He walked around the desk, grabbed my arm, pulled me out of the chair, and before I could protest, I was bent over the desk, his hand meeting my ass. The heat from the smack radiated through the material, and I should have been upset that I was being manhandled. Instead, my pussy clenched, and I felt myself grow damp. How could I be mad at this man and turned on at the same time?

He crowded behind me, his erection pushing into my ass, and the moan echoed off the walls. I found myself pushing back into him, wiggling, wanting to be taken.

"Ah, that's it. My girl thinks her attitude will stop me from claiming what's mine. She doesn't want to give in, but she will." Speed thrust his hips, and I moaned again from the pressure of his cock. I wanted to feel the skin on skin, but the material of our clothing was an unwanted barrier.

He backed away, and I felt his weight loss until my skirt was pushed to my waist and his hand smoothed over my ass cheeks to slide between my legs, cupping me.

"Babe, you're wet already, and I'd love to experiment with what got you to this point, but my dick is aching to be surrounded by your tight pussy."

The rip of material and my thong was out of his way. With the sound of a zipper, my stomach tightened, anticipating what would come next. The wait wasn't long as his weight hit, and his cock entered me in one hard thrust. I gasped, then pushed back and moaned as my head was jerked back by him grabbing my hair.

"Loving the ponytail, babe." His words came out strained. "No more getting pissy because I had a blowjob. This is where my dick wants to be and will be from now on." He pulled out, tightened the grip on my hair, and slammed back in. "That's it, babe. Feel it, your pussy tightening, not wanting to let go. It wants my dick, only mine. Tell me, Sami, say it. Let me give you what you need." The dirty talk, the fullness, everything, I was dooming myself to heartbreak, and I couldn't stop it as I gave him what he wanted.

"Fuck me, I want you to fuck me, damn it," I barely got the words out before he snapped. My head was pulled back, his teeth nipped at my neck, and as he pounded into me, my mind shut down, and I felt. Felt him. Just him.

We crested together, and his full weight slumped against me as my head lay on the desk. When our breathing leveled, he lifted off, bringing me with him, and sat me in the chair. I watched as he tucked himself back in his jeans, his shirt following, neither of us speaking. The kiss on my forehead had me blinking, then he walked around the desk. When he reached the door, he looked over his shoulder.

"Babe, you might want to fix your clothes before you come out. You've got the fucked on my desk look going on." The door opened and closed as he left.

Chapter Eighteen

Sami

The woman who looked back at me in the mirror was not the same as the one from just a week ago. The green in her eyes shined, her cheeks were rosy, and she had bed head. The woman looked well-loved, and she should since she'd spent the night being ravished, fucked, and even had love made to her slowly as the sun rose that morning.

I loved the look of the new woman, and I hoped she stayed. I blinked, pushed the hair away from my face, turned toward the shower, and started the spray, letting it only warm for a minute before stepping in.

After my shower, I dressed, made the bed, and prepared to go down to start breakfast. Carly would be over, Ally would get up, and my dad and brother would arrive soon after.

My thoughts went to the man who left my bed this morning. Speed had spent every night in my bed since the night at the club. I'd sat at my desk a while after he'd left the office until I had no choice, I was the manager and had to take care of business. When I'd walked out into the club, it was like being under a microscope, eyes on me, smirks on every man associated with Black Hawk, including the man who had caused it. He was a smug bastard, but I couldn't help the inwardly smile then, and I couldn't help now.

"Someone got laid last night, again, I might add. He's determined to get you, either on your own or by spoiling you with sex nightly until you fall in a puddle of goo." Carly laughed as she walked into the kitchen.

"I didn't hear you even come in." How would I not have my dad and brother asking questions if I couldn't stay focused?

"You were somewhere else, maybe with a certain biker?" She wagged her eyebrows up and down.

"Not one word. I mean it. I haven't talked with Ally about Speed yet. I don't need my brother and dad going into a protective mode or worse, murder. I want to be able to tell them and not have them go off. You know they will." It hadn't helped that right before Speed left this morning, he reminded me I was now down to two days left of my week. I wanted my daughter to have a father, but a part of me still didn't want to risk myself. It had nothing to do with him. He spent time with Ally before she went to bed, in the morning, he fixed breakfast and ate with her before he left. And that only made me feel more like shit for holding off telling her.

When the two were together, there was no doubt they were already close and cared for each other. I was the one holding back, the one with doubts about forever with a man I was still getting to know, and the one who was afraid to let her feeling be known for fear of rejection.

"Earth to Sami."

"I swear if you don't stop, I'm going to slap the crap out of you. For someone who, a few days ago, suffered from issues with MCs, you sure have changed your tune."

The smile left her face, and I felt like shit, it wasn't her fault I was nervous about discussing any of this with my dad. "Sorry, uncalled for." I moved around the kitchen to stay busy if I stopped, there was a good chance of a breakdown.

"You're happy, which makes me happy. And I know you are worried about what your dad is going to say but, Sami, he wants you happy too. With all the crap going on at Haven, you being here, I think you will be surprised how he reacts to everything. I promise not to spill before you get the chance to tell him. I'll even try not to kill Reed when he starts in on his relentless teasing of us. The man is older than we are, yet he reverts back to eight when he is around us." She was right about that, Reed had always been a pain in our ass growing up.

Ally was dressed when she walked into the kitchen, "When are Grandpa and Uncle Reed getting here?" She bounced where she stood, looking between Carly and me.

"Excited are you, short girl?" Yet another nickname that had Ally giggling.

"Yep, is Speed coming too?" Carly looked at me and

smirked. Yeah, I couldn't wait long to talk with my dad, Ally would spill all if she had an opening.

"No, sweetie, he's busy today. Today is about your grandpa, okay?"

"Okay. But will he come for a sleepover tonight?" I glared at Carly when she laughed, which only made her laugh harder. But before more could be said, we heard the sound of bikes, and Ally took off for the front door. Seemed my dad and brother had arrived.

"What's going on, Sami?" My dad came in the back door. I'd come in the house to get everyone something to drink while we waited for dinner to be ready. The day had gone smoothly, and Ally hadn't even mentioned Speed in front of him or my brother. I needed to come clean before she did, I just hadn't found the right time to talk with him.

Wild Bill stood patiently waiting for me to answer him. "Nothing, everything is going great here. A little sad you can only stay tonight and have to go back in the morning, but I understand." He'd planned to stay two days, but something had happened before he left Haven, he wouldn't say what because "it's club business," the standard response was given, so they needed to get back.

And I was running out of time.

"You've been acting normal, and the key to that is acting. Something is going on, and I want to know right now." He was digging in, I knew, when his arms crossed over his chest. He wasn't going to give up, and I cracked. We were alone in the house; Carly, Reed, and Ally were outside.

Reed had the grill going, and Carly and Ally were kicking a ball around in the yard. Might as well give it up, he wouldn't kill his own daughter, maybe.

"Dad, I need to tell you who—" The doorbell cut me off, and my dad headed for the door. I sighed, when he came back, I would just blurt it out, then deal when it was over.

"Who are you?" I rushed out of the kitchen at my dad's tone and slid to a stop when Speed looked over my dad's head at me. This was so not going to be good. Speed left this morning because he knew my dad was due. He said he'd give me time.

"Kane Weston, Enforcer at Black Hawk, call me Speed."

"They know I'm visiting, I called and cleared it. Maybe you need to be better at retaining info." My dad's voice changed into a club's president voice. The one that said, "Don't fuck with me." I tried to give Speed the "what are you doing" stare, but he ignored me, and when he spoke, I seriously thought my head was going to explode.

"Yeah, we know you are here."

"Then why are you standing at my daughter's door?

"My dad asked you a question, asshole. This is my sister's house?" My head turned when Reed spoke, I hadn't even heard him come through the house. Bells, everyone was going to start wearing fucking bells.

Chapter Nineteen

Speed

I'd chuckle at the look on Sami's face if her dad weren't standing there, looking like he was ready to go down. She favored him, the dark hair and green eyes, but the facial features and height, she must've inherited from her mother.

Wild Bill was a large barrel-chested man who stood at least six foot five. Before I could answer his last question, I watched another large man walk toward the door. Had to be the brother, Reed. He took after Wild Bill in everything except the hair and eyes. I imagined the sandy blond hair and blue eyes were shared with his mother.

They waited for me to speak. When I came, I intended to meet her dad, giving Sami support if she needed it. She was supposed to talk to him and tell him about me being Ally's dad. She hadn't, and when Wild Bill opened the door, he might have asked who I was, but his eyes had told a different story before they went blank again. One of acknowledgment. He saw the resemblance like everyone else.

So since he knew or suspected, I decided to verify it for him, using the word 'My' once again—for him and the brother.

"Yeah, and this is *MY* woman's house and *MY* daughter's." The brother's eyes narrowed, Sami turned pale, and when I looked at Wild Bill, his face was blank, then he nodded his head and stepped back.

"Come on in, Speed, let's go out back and have a beer and talk. Seems my dau… your woman was holding back some information." He walked by Sami, "I'll get that from her later." I followed, and as I passed Sami, I stopped and kissed her forehead, then continued behind Wild Bill, leaving her and Reed standing there.

We stepped out the back, and I was immediately hit by a tiny body. "Speed, you came back. I missed you at breakfast." I bent down and hugged my daughter, who had no issue letting anything out of the bag. The back door opened, and Sami and Reed joined us.

"Reed and I seem to be the last to know what's going on. Imagine you know how that feels." He looked at Carly while he spoke, probably because of the smirk on her face. "Sami, you girls go in the house and finish the rest of the stuff for dinner. Reed, Speed, and I will sit down here and watch the grill." Sami glared at me but nodded to acknowledge her dad, then she took Ally's hand and headed inside with Carly right behind them.

Reed reached into the cooler, handed his dad and me a beer, and we sat in the chairs at the corner of the patio.

"Let's get right down to it." I pointed with my beer for him to start. "Sami kept your name from us no matter how much I badgered her. But I could kick my own ass for not figuring it out. I knew your dad from the military, you look just like him, and my granddaughter is the spitting image of you both. Don't know how I missed that shit. Anyway, I'm not going to ask how this happened because I'm a dad, we still like to imagine that our daughters don't have sex, and I like that little fantasy. You'll understand that when Ally becomes a teen." Reed laughed, but it didn't last. "Don't laugh, the way you whore around I keep waiting for some woman to come by yelling about you being the baby's daddy." I had to bite the inside of my mouth to keep myself from laughing.

"I don't want to like you, but I think I'm going to. Any man who comes to the door of a woman's house to confront her dad and brother without thinking of getting his ass kicked is a brave motherfucker or a stupid one. There is no in-between. Since you're wearing that Enforcer patch, I'm going with brave motherfucker.

"That being said, you must remember that I am a bigger and meaner bastard. I will kill you and bury the body where no one will find it, and if they do, they'll have to put the pieces together to identify you. Now, why don't you tell me what's going on between you two? Ally isn't calling you daddy, so she doesn't know, why is that?" The man never blinked while he spoke. Not once had he diverted his eyes away from me.

"I've been getting to know my daughter. I'm letting Sami think she is getting her way. I would have left the military sooner if I had known she existed. You only need to know that she is mine, and I protect what's mine. Your daughter is a little trickier, but I got that handled."

Reed shook his head. "Really, you got her handled. Even Prez over here," he pointed his beer at Wild Bill, "had a hard time with that when she was growing up. She's stubborn, and sometimes if you push her too much, you end up with scars." He lifted the hair off his forehead to show a scar at the hairline. "I walked into her room while she and Carly were having a sleepover. They were dancing, and she threw a school book at me when she saw me. Clocked my ass good before I could duck."

"I won't waste your time with bullshit. Sami is mine, and so is Ally. By next week, they will be living in my house on the Black Hawk compound. They've got two families right now, Black Hawk and Haven. You know as well as I know any enemies get wind of that, and it will be used against both clubs. We know you are having issues internally, Stroker told me to tell you to call him. Our clubs may not have seen eye to eye before, but we have a reason to work toward that now.

"Since the next time you come, they will be at the compound, I want to extend the invite to you that you're welcome there. I know Sami and Ally would like it. I'm not going to tell you what's going on as far as Sami goes because I haven't told her. Once I do, I'm sure she will let you know." I finished my beer while Wild Bill cocked his head at me. When he straightened, he smiled.

"I am going to like you. I like what I see in you." The door opened, and Sami stepped out and looked between us.

"Food is done." Reed finished pulling the meat off the grill and started for the house, and Wild Bill stood.

"You joining us?" Sami asked me, and I shook my head.

"No, babe. Going to let you and Ally visit with your dad and brother. I got to get back."

"Okay."

Wild Bill watched the play, I knew he was evaluating us together. I also knew Sami was banking that I wouldn't put her on the spot with her dad there. Her eyes informed me I was right when they flashed fire as I stepped up and kissed her forehead.

"Forty-eight hours, babe. Don't forget." I shook Wild Bill's hand, went through the house, hugged my daughter bye, and told her I would see her soon.

I looked over my shoulder as I drove down the street, Sami stood in the doorway watching. I'd go back to the compound, and I would stay away from her. She'd either come to me willingly, or I would come back and get her. Made no difference, the clock was ticking down, and I wanted my family together.

Sami

When I closed the front door, I felt him behind me. I turned and fell into his open arms, resting my cheek on his chest.

"God, Dad, he confuses me."

"Do you love him, baby? Not because of Ally, because of you."

"Yes."

"Then what's the problem, Sami?"

"I don't know if he does, not for me, but because I'm Ally's mother. I need it to be for me, Dad."

"Know what I see?" He moved me back so he could look into my eyes.

"What?"

"A man who sees what he wants and is going to have it, no matter what. Don't protest, I'm not done. I also saw how he looked at you, which I imagine is the same way I looked at your mother. When you look at him, it's the same way your mother looked at me. You need to tell Ally, Sami. She needs to know. Her heart is already his. I'd never seen her look so happy until he walked outside earlier. You make your own mind up, but don't keep her from him. Now, anyone else going to stop by that's going to hold my dinner up?"

I chuckled at his lame attempt to lighten the mood, put my arm around his waist, and led us to the kitchen.

"What was the forty-eight-hour business?"

My dad listened as I explained the ultimatum given and told him I didn't know if I was going to ignore it or not. He laughed and squeezed me.

"Totally like him. I will dance at your wedding if he can get you to do what he wants."

"Seriously, you laughed at a man steamrolling over your daughter. Some father you are." I pulled away and acted indignant at him. He pulled me back into his arms.

"Please, you wouldn't even let something like that bother you. But you're bothered. Tells me, next time I visit will be at the Black Hawk compound." He squeezed me and stepped away to sit at the table by Ally, leaving me standing there with no idea what to do.

There was plenty of time, I decided, and sat down at the table. I'd enjoy the rest of the visit with my dad and brother, then after they were gone, I'd think about what to do about Speed, not like he would really come and haul us to the compound.

Chapter Twenty

Speed

"You know this is fucked up, Speed?"

"You agreed, so shut up, Flirt."

"Because you told our dads. What are you, five?" I smirked at Crusher as I opened the door to the building, and he flipped me off.

"Jesus, I didn't like coming in here when I had to."

"Devil, you're just afraid they're going to realize they are smarter than you." That earned me another finger.

"Damn, was everything always so fucking small?"

"That's a bad word, Jag." He laughed but still flipped me off.

"Speed, you're going to owe us big for this shit."

"Keep thinking that, Coast, if it helps you get through it." Double fingers. I felt the love as we stopped in front of the door.

"Get ready, brothers, you may never be the same when this is over." I opened the door to the big room and walked in with my brothers following behind.

When we entered, heads turned, and a few eyes got big, not every day did six huge tattooed bikers walk into a classroom. Mrs. Elderman greeted us and pointed to the table where we would be.

She was the first one I saw as she sat with her back to us. I'd called to check the time the day before and had a nice discussion with Mrs. Elderman. She'd informed me that Ally wouldn't be the only child there without a daddy, some were single parents, and the moms couldn't attend because they had to work, then others whose fathers couldn't take off. So yeah, I steamrolled my brothers.

I hadn't been back to see Sami since I went by to meet her dad. I couldn't go without talking with her, though, so I called her each night. That's how I knew she wouldn't be here today. Ally told her last night she didn't want to go to the party, but Sami wouldn't let her back out of it. She told Ally you didn't let anyone dictate what you could do just because things weren't tied up in a nice little bow. If my daughter took after her mother, she'd be a strong woman able to stand independently if needed. Like that would ever happen.

Sami's time was up tomorrow, and I needed her to come on her own to me. I'd never needed someone as I needed her. I'd realized too late that the ultimatum I set would crush me too if she blew me off. I was banking on what I'd seen in her eyes when she looked at me.

We were almost to the table when a little girl across from us leaned in, that's when Ally raised her head and saw us, the smile that followed was worth the shit I heard from the others yesterday when I mentioned this. They came anyway, it was what brothers did, they'd always have my back. We reached her table, and she jumped in my arms when I opened them to her.

"You came." She hugged me tight, and then I sat her down. "You all came." She smiled at them, her eyes glistened just the slightest, and I'd remember this moment forever when I looked at my brothers. I'd remind them of the day one little girl had stolen their hearts, just like she'd done mine.

We made our introductions, and each took a seat by a kid. I shook my head when I noticed Flirt sat with the only boy at the table. He looked at us and smirked. At first, the kids had been shy, but it only took Ally to tell me what I was doing wrong to have the other kids do the same.

"Not like that, Speed. You got to put a little glue, then press the noodle in it."

"Sure thing, darlin'."

Crusher chuckled beside me until the little girl he sat by chimed in. "At least your daddy fill-in (the title they deemed us) can use the scissors."

"If they made the da…" Ally looked over at Crusher and smiled, "dang things weren't made to fit big hands."

"Please, Aaron and I didn't have any trouble cutting ours out." Flirt patted the kid on the back and got a smile for his effort. I had to admit it looked good. Instead of folding out dolls, they did a motorcycle.

"How come you didn't cut me out a bike? I don't like dolls," Ally told me, and the others hadn't dared to look at me, but I'd heard their snickers.

"Next time, okay?" When she got quiet, I looked down at her. "What?"

"You going to be here for my next daddy party?" The kids continued to talk, but my brothers looked at me, my brows cocked, they hadn't had to say a word. It was time to tell her, but not in a classroom full of parents and kids.

"I will be there for your party or any other time you need me. Always." She didn't answer, she just sighed and leaned into me, placing her head on my arm.

We'd made faces on paper plates with noodles and cut construction paper to fan out into dolls, but the kids made the experience enjoyable.

After crafts, we ate lunch with them and had cake. Overall the time had ended on a good note. Parents hugged their kids goodbye and filed out of the classroom. The kids who'd sat with my brothers gave them hugs and told them bye. I wished I had my phone out to take pictures of their faces when the kids had done that. It would have been great entertainment at the next Church.

"See ya, darlin'." I stood back up from hugging Ally.

"Yous doing a sleepover tonight with Momma?"

"Not tonight, Ally. Soon, okay?"

"'K." She sat back in her chair, sighed, and touched the doll we cut out. I knew what she wanted; I wanted the same thing.

By the time I'd gotten outside, the guys were standing by their bikes, all but Coast. While I walked toward the others, I searched the parking lot and found him talking with one of the men who had been at the party. The man looked familiar, but I couldn't place him.

"Whose Coast talking to?"

I received shrugs as we watched Coast walk toward us and get on his bike.

"Who was that he looked familiar?" I asked, and Coast chuckled.

"Bert Samson."

"The mayor's son?" Devil asked.

"And Benji's dad. I asked Mari, the little girl I sat with, to point Benji out. So when I walked out and was waiting on you guys, I saw Bert come out. Thought I'd have a little talk with him." Coast revved his bike, ready to leave.

"And?" I asked.

"Told him to teach his kid that males were to be nice to girls. And added that the next time Benji said ugly shit to Ally, as his dad, he would be the one taught how to treat a woman by Ally's dad and uncles."

We laughed and pulled out of the parking lot.

Sami

I paced and worried so much at the club that Tank and Perry teamed up on me. They volunteered to stay past their shifts and close Soft Tails if I would just go home. It seemed I had gotten on their nerves. Whatever.

When I dropped Ally off today for school and her party, she asked again if she could just go to Mrs. Mayson's house. I wanted to let her do it, but I couldn't let her think that it was okay to be excluded because you were different. Still, I checked with Mrs. Elderman, and Ally wouldn't be the only one without a parent there. Ally gave in, went to her seat, and I went to work.

She spotted me when she was brought out with the other car riders. The smile plastered on her face told me she was happy to see me. The bouncing in the backseat told me the day hadn't been so bad.

"He came, Momma. They all came. We made faces on plates and cut out dolls, and he said next time we'd do a bike like Aaron got to do, and he'd come to my parties."

When she stopped to breathe, I asked, "Who, sweetie?"

"Speed and his friends, they all came, and we didn't have to sit by ourselves and make our things. We called them the fill-in daddies." I imagined the six big bikers had been a hit and didn't even know it.

I looked in the rearview mirror, she was so happy as she ran her hand over the face she'd made on the plate.

"When is Daddy going to live with us all the time?"

"What?"

"Speed, he's my daddy, when will we all live together?" When I looked back in the mirror, she was looking at me.

"You know Speed's your daddy?" Everyone had been careful not to say anything in front of her until we could figure out how to go about it.

"Yes." No pause, no hesitation from her.

"How do you know?"

"He has my face."

Well, wasn't that simple.

"Yes, he does."

Chapter Twenty-One

Speed

I'd closed the door to the room the guys had helped me finish when I heard the car pull up. I made it downstairs and opened the front door when a pair of arms wrapped around my legs and another pair around my neck.

"What's wrong?" My daughter was attached to my legs, and her mother had me around the neck, and my chest tightened on what it could mean.

"You went to the school. You had your friends go too. You made a doll out of paper and promised a bike next time." I looked down into Sami's eyes when she stepped back.

"Okay, and you drove out here to tell me that. I was there."

Tears filled her eyes, and I would have panicked if she

hadn't smiled. "I know, I know, I'm rambling. She told me about her day with you, she made it simple. It had all been so simple."

"Babe, you got to give me a clue here."

Ally let go of my legs and looked up at me, "Daddy, it's because you got my face." Then she walked into the house like she'd been there before. And her mother was right—it was that simple.

"Did she just call me—"

"Daddy. She has known all along, Kane. I guess she waited for us to catch up."

"You know you aren't leaving here, right? You came here, and now you can't leave."

"I hadn't planned to. We're home, Kane if you want us?"

"You got me a bike, Daddy!"

"You didn't." I took Sami's hand and pulled her into the house and up the stairs, where we found our daughter in the room my brothers and I had just finished. Her room.

"Oh my God. Did you do all this for her?" Sami walked into the room and turned in circles.

"We finished it today. Remember, your time wasn't up till tomorrow." I only had time to brace myself and catch her as she ran to me. She pulled me down and kissed me.

"I love you, Kane Weston." Words I had waited for and had seen in her eyes.

"Babe, I love you." I bent and took her mouth, she melted into me, but the giggling had me pulling back. Ally sat on the seat of the bike that made up one side of her bed frame.

It was the first bikes my brothers and I had built in the garage. We assembled a bed and made the sides bikes, our first job of Sons of Black Hawk Custom Bikes, these just didn't have any working parts. The headboard we fixed looked like a garage, so when you stood at the bottom of the bed, it looked as though the bikes pulled out of the garage. That project had been the dads' contribution. The room we painted and furnished for a girl. It'd been an experience, but when Shakes had found out what was going on, she helped us pick out the things. Her contribution had been the pink comforter on the bed to go with the pink we'd painted the bikes.

"You did this for me?"

"Sure did."

"I love you, Daddy."

Sami squeezed my hand.

"I love you, baby girl."

As I stood in that room, holding my woman's hand and watching my daughter pretend to ride a bike, I thought of the first time I walked into this house when I got back. My life without my dad hadn't started that day at all—it started almost five and a half years ago when I stared into green eyes across the room—I just hadn't realized then how much that one night with Sami would come to mean to me.

Epilogue

Crusher

When I walked in the door to Speed's house with the box in my hand, I stopped short at the sight in front of me. Deputy Sweetass, as I referred to her now, was bent unpacking a box. The closet door was open as she pulled items out and folded them, placing them in the open box to the side.

Juggling the box so I could hold it with one hand while I adjusted my crotch didn't work, and the box hit the floor, which caused her to jump and stand. She turned toward me, and her brown eyes flashed. A prickly little thing was what she was.

"Perv. You better hope nothing breakable was in that box, or Sami will kick your ass." Her eyes lit, and she smirked. "Not that I wouldn't enjoy watching her do it." She turned back to her task, and I picked up the box and headed toward the kitchen. She didn't say another word to me, but she didn't bend over either. Squatting instead to grab the next coat out of the box.

I'm a grown damn man who would be taking over for my dad as president of Black Hawk MC. I should act like it, but the woman drove every ounce of maturity out of me when she was around. That is probably why when I walked past her, I grabbed a handful of ass and squeezed, then kept walking even as I felt something hit the back of my head. The woman had good aim. I'd take the hit because she had a better ass, and touching it was worth whatever she dished out. A man had to weigh what was important.

"Seriously, she will shoot you one day with her gun." Speed stood in the kitchen doorway and had evidently witnessed the exchange. "Going to tell me now what is up with you two?"

I shook my head; my friend was happy. Good for him. Family life suited him.

"Did I miss where we grew vaginas and started gossiping? Should we schedule time from getting the shop up and running to go shop for shoes?" I smirked as he narrowed his eyes at me. We're a damn motorcycle club, for God's sake.

"We could go on a shopping trip for shoes. I need some new riding boots." Jag shrugged his shoulders when we all turned and looked at him. "What, like you don't shop for shit? Do clothes and stuff pop in your fucking drawers and closets when they need to be replaced?"

The back door opened, and Flirt walked in carrying a box overflowing with toys. "Thank fuck Spider likes boy shit because I don't think I could have even touched this if there were dolls and frilly shit in the box." He sat it down on the table and pointed his finger at the rest of us. "I mean it. She's the only little girl allowed. The rest of you fuckers have kids; they better be boys. We may not get lucky the next time, and I refuse to play fucking dolls."

Sami, Coast, and Devil came downstairs and walked into the kitchen. Coast and Devil with lips pursed and Sami smirking.

"What you smiling at, baby?" Speed placed his arm over her shoulder when she walked up to him, drawing her closer. Fuck, he was a goner.

"I told them not to open a box, and being men, they thought I was trying to hide sexy underwear or sex toys," she rolled her eyes, "so they opened the box." She laughed at their groans.

"Come on, Sami. We weren't that bad."

"Please, shouldn't the devil be used to fire?" Sami laughed louder. Now she had our curiosity about what my brothers found.

"Give it up, girl. Spill your guts." Her green eyes shined at me, full of humor.

"Well, okay, since you twisted my arm."

Before she could go on, Coast moved closer to her. "Don't ruin our image. These fuckers are relentless."

"Ah, no. You're bad boy biker imposters." Speed glared down at her. Then smiled when she patted his chest,

"Not you, baby. You're the baddest of the bunch."

"Goddamn, I'm going to be sick." I chuckled and looked down the hall at Carly as she checked the pockets of a leather jacket she pulled from the closet. She folded the jacket, placed it in the box, and then opened the paper.

"They opened the box and stepped back as if it was on fire. It contained bathroom items and feminine products." We all laughed at Coast's and Devil's expense. My laughter died as I watched Carly's face go pale, her head raised, and she looked at me. The paper feathered to the floor as she dropped it and turned for the door. She ran out before I even moved toward her.

"Carly, wait!" I raced out of the kitchen to the front door just as she cranked her bike and pulled out.

"What the fuck happened?" Speed stood behind me, and we watched her ride until she was out of sight.

"She was packing that box and read something she found in a pocket when she checked." We turned around at the gasp and the group "Fuck" that was yelled by the others. Sami stood there, note in one hand, the other over her mouth. Flirt, Coast, Devil, and Jag stood behind her, and the look they wore was one of shock.

"What is it?" Speed and I said together.

When she looked at Speed, Sami's green eyes filled with tears, and she held out the paper. When he reached her, she placed it in his hand, and we read it as he held the paper between us.

"Holy fuck." I turned back and walked out the door. I didn't know what, who, or why about the letter, but the others would figure it out.

Carly wasn't going to be happy with me following her. She may not want me, but something told me she would need me.

Acknowledgements

Thanks to all who believed I could write something people actually wanted to read.

And to those who are/or will read this—a huge thanks for taking a chance on a new author—you are what makes the grueling hours' worth it.

Carson

About the Author

Carson Mackenzie enjoys writing romance with a real feel inside the stories. She writes with the belief not every man is a jerk and not every woman needs saving.

Carson lives in the South with one of her sons, a Great Dane and two adopted shelter dogs that keep the household in line. Books have always been a part of her life. There is nothing better to her than curling up and relaxing with a good story and losing herself in someone else's world for a few hours.

Writing stories and growing as an author with each book is her goal. She wants to reach the level where a reader knows when they see her name, they can trust in the fact there will be a good story as they flip through the pages.

Carson's been her writing journey for a few years. As she's finally starting to settle in, her only regret is she hadn't started sooner.

To stay up to date with Carson – visit her Website or sign up for her Newsletter.

Books by Carson Mackenzie

Black Hawk MC

Haven MC

Moose's Regret
Hawk's Bounty
Keg's Revelation

Desert Phoenix MC

Desert Phoenix Rising

Standalones

Her Way or No Way
two paths One destiny

Boxed Sets

Black Hawk MC Books 1-3
Black Hawk MC Books 4-7
Haven MC Books 1-3

Lightning Source UK Ltd.
Milton Keynes UK
UKHW041122281222
414464UK00019B/360